MY SECRET WEAPON

WEAPON

THE STOP LOSS SYSTEM

First published 1997

British Library Cataloguing in Publication Data. A
catalogue record for this book is available from the British
Library.

ISBN 0 948035 71 4

Cover and Book Design by Michael Firth
Typeset by Don Wright

Published by:
Rushmere Wynne Group PLC
4-5 Harmill, Grovebury Road,
Leighton Buzzard
Bedfordshire LU7 8FF
Tel: 01525 853726
Fax: 01525 852037

Printed by:
BPC Wheatons Ltd.
Hennock Road,
Marsh Barton,
Exeter EX2 8RP

MY SECRET WEAPON

THE STOP LOSS SYSTEM

by

Michael Walters

Rushmere Wynne
England

Other books by Michael Walters

How To Make A Killing In Penny Shares
How To Make A Killing In The Share Jungle
How To Make A Killing In New Issues
How To Profit From Your Personal Equity Plan
How To Profit From The Coming Share Boom
How To Make A Killing In The AIM

CONTENTS

PREFACE

The idea for this book has been kicking around in my mind for a couple of years. The ability to write regularly in a national newspaper gives me privileged access to investors. It brings a heavy responsibility, not just to pick holes in sophisticated City schemes – important though that is sometimes – but to try to do something constructive, to help readers. That is why, though I am not required to do so, I choose to run a share tipping column in the *Daily Mail*, when I think the time is right.

Happily, it has been successful through the mid-nineties. If I start getting it too wrong, too often, I will stop. I am grateful for the nice letters readers sometimes send me. And frustrated to learn from others that I am not really getting through clearly to everyone, especially when it comes to selling shares. It worries me that, if the market should collapse, my efforts to help people make money will end up having the effect of costing them money, because they have bought on my tips, but failed to sell at the right time because I have not managed to get the message across properly.

It is not possible to say everything I wish in a newspaper column. Hence this book. It also arises from an uneasy feeling that many investment pundits have become too cosy a part of the system. They are too divorced from the every day way things work for investors who may only have a few thousand pounds to play with, and who live and move in a system a world away from the City insider.

> Clever investment theories may sound good, but they are not practical for smaller players who may struggle to understand them.

Clever investment theories may sound good, but they are not practical for smaller players, who may struggle to understand them. And they rarely have much to say about selling shares.

This book claims no great sophistication, but draws on 35 years of small-time share trading and writing about investment. It tries to offer a practical answer, a system which is not always workable, but which everyone can understand and adapt to their own needs. It works well most of the time, but is not infallible.

I am slightly embarrassed that it contains so many examples from my *Daily Mail* columns, but they are important. They are there because I am trying to deal with the real world as it unfolds before the private investor. The examples draw on actual advice I have offered readers of my investment columns, week by week, for better or worse, using real share tips, real prices, in real time. They show how the system panned out, as we went along, and how I got it wrong sometimes. But they do rely on real, practical experience, not the benefits of hindsight or the infallible genius of empty theory.

I would like to thank the *Daily Mail* for permission to use extracts from my columns and David Linton of Updata software for supplying the charts to illustrate the points I want to make.

This is a short book. I hope investors consider it worthwhile. I have written it, not to make money, but because I feel a sense of duty to the investors who read my columns, and a gratitude for those who have been kind enough to say nice things about them. I am particularly grateful to my publisher and friend, Tony Drury of Rushmere Wynne, for letting me write it. Good luck.

INTRODUCTION

Inertia rules, OK? It drives me to distraction. Wherever you go in the investment world, there is someone trotting out the same old line – long term investment is what makes money. Short term trading is no good. Buy, sit tight, and all will be well. Something will turn up. You will make much more money by being patient than those sharp lads who leap in and out, trying to make a quick killing all of the time. They run up heavy trading costs which gobble up any profits – even if they manage to pick the right stocks.

Long term good, short term bad. It is a marvellous mantra, the City's favourite investment formula. It comes complete with a vague in-built air of moral superiority. Somehow, it seems, anything else is vaguely improper, slightly suspect. It smacks of greed, the get-rich-quick notion.

Inertia rules, OK?

Hardly anyone ever seems to challenge this approach. After all, who would want to align themselves with the quick-buck spivs? And whereas it is easy to blow the dust off old record books, go back to the beginning of the century, and demonstrate that share prices simply get better and better through the years if you live long enough, it is tougher to stand up in public and try to prove it might have been smarter to sell near the peaks and buy again near the troughs.

No-one is ready to believe that you would actually manage to do it. How would you know when to sell? And when to buy again? That takes some difficult decisions. You might not get it right. Far better to play safe, sit tight, and let time wash away the urge for action. You will not go wrong that way. Inertia rules, ok?

Buffett – The Genius

If proof were needed that patience pays, fans can always point to the Warren Buffett way. The chairman of a holding company called Berkshire Hathaway, he did not become the second-richest man in the world by leaping in and out of the stock market. The Sage of Omaha has made billions by buying, sitting, and watching. The stock-picker supreme, he has become an investment legend. His 1996 chairman's letter to shareholders explains that in the 32 years since he took over at Berkshire Hathaway, per share book value has advanced from $19 to $19,011, a rate of 23.8% annual compound growth. That may understate the true performance. But it is hard to understate Buffett's brilliance.

Buffett is a genius, an extraordinary exception. Do it

the Buffett way, play it long, and you cannot go wrong. Or can you?

It sounds simple the way the legions of long term investment apologists tell it. You want to sing like Sinatra? Get up and do it. Hit a golf ball like Tiger Woods? Buy a set of clubs, a few balls and whack 'em for a while. Write like Tom Stoppard? Sit down and do it.

You can't, of course. It is not as simple as that. Like Sinatra, Woods, or Stoppard, old Warren has something special, something you cannot pick up by reading the instruction book. He really does have a touch of genius. You can learn from him, just as you might learn from analysing the way any successful individual does what they do. But to suggest that copying what they do will produce the same results for you is plainly nonsense.

> Buffett is special, very special. His approach is far more sophisticated than the popular perception which feeds on his nicely home-spun sayings.

Investing the Buffett way may make some sort of sense to you. If it appeals, go for it. You are unlikely to be able to emulate the master's achievements. And just because it works for him, that does not necessarily mean it is the way for everyone.

Even Buffett makes mistakes. He admits it. Without his talent for spotting the best companies, and what are now his massive resources to research businesses and ability to chat to almost anyone from the US President down as he weighs an investment decision, are you going to pick long term winners every time?

Buffett is special, very special. His approach is far more sophisticated than the popular perception which feeds on his nicely home-spun sayings. Just because buying and holding works outstandingly well for him, that does not necessarily mean that it will work for everyone else. How can you be so sure that the stocks you have picked have the qualities to endure and prosper? Spotting long term winners is not easy. Relatively few companies are that reliable.

No matter how carefully you choose your prospective winner, can you be sure you have not made a mistake? At some point, you have to consider the possibility. Then you have to decide whether to stick, and risk going for bust. Or whether to cut your losses, and walk away while you still have something left. Not easy, that, if you are small private investor, trying to build a nest-egg for your future. Old Warren has a few billions working for him. Buffett has a bit of a buffer, should he get it wrong.

In fact, he recognises that direct investment is not for everyone. He argues that most investors are better off owning shares through a Tracker fund which seeks to duplicate the stock market indices. Pick one with minimal charges, he says, and after deducting fees and expenses, you are sure to beat the majority of investment professionals. Quite right.

Do not be blinded. Please note that the investment guru is suggesting you pick a passive fund, one which is not actively managed by any of those smart City types who are so keen to suggest you let them look after your money for the long term.

These are the folk who love the idea of long term, value investment, and who are knee-deep in stock analysis systems and so on. Yet, as the master suggests, the majority just fail to keep pace with the average market performance. Their understanding of the more sophisticated aspects of investment (and their big fat

> Do not be blinded by the legend of Warren Buffett.

flow of inside information) does not help them much. Especially when the management company which employs them chooses to divert so much of the investor's precious cash into paying these people their enormous salaries and inflated bonuses.

So do not be blinded by the legend of Warren Buffett. Few of the big investors who pay lip service to his ideas can make them work as well as he can. Of course he is wonderful, almost impossible to fault on his own terms. You hardly need an antidote to Buffett himself, just to the way in which he has been adopted as the symbol of an altogether less sensible cult of long term investment for all, come what may. What old Warren says makes sense – from his perspective. Your circumstances are different, and that may mean you have to play it differently.

If you are a small investor, ready to take a little risk in the hope of making something worthwhile in the stock market, inertia is no good. A steady long term increase in value on a little pile of money means that, after inflation, you still have a tidy packet of peanuts. You cannot afford to be a patient, long term, ever-so-serious player. You need to be a punter. You need to be an active investor. And to be a successful active investor, it is imperative that you control your risk, and limit your losses.

◆ ◆ ◆

Exploiting The Opportunities

Try a dash of simple common sense. Buy shares when they are low, and sell when they are high. That is the way to make money in the stock market. In investment terms, it hardly gets any simpler than that.

It is hard to imagine that anyone would argue with such a basic proposition. And yet . . . and yet this simple view has become cluttered by the cult of the long term investor, cluttered so badly that many seem not to notice that it obscures other tried and tested investment ideas.

Markets and individual shares have their bad days,

and their good days. They have bad weeks, bad months, sometimes bad years. It must make sense to sell when prices are high, and buy when they are low. No-one buys the whole market, but the general mood does influence the price of individual shares. And individual shares can move sharply up or down, whether markets are good or bad.

Prices do not move of their own accord. They move because people are buying and selling. Some people are better informed than others, and use that information – legally or illegally – to buy and sell. There are always investors who know better than the rest. They always deal. Whether the authorities can catch them or not, insiders are always buying and selling. Watch carefully enough, and shares often give the game away. The active investor can watch prices, and read the message they are sending. No system is infallible. But when it comes to selling, price movements can be remarkably instructive and revealing.

The Crucial Issue – Selling Shares

The sensible active investor is the investor who seeks to reduce exposure to risk. A simple Stop Loss system which involves selling when a price falls a pre-determined amount – say 10% or 20% – can reduce risk considerably.

So often in investment advice, selling seems to have been tossed out of the reckoning. Enormous effort is devoted to identifying how and when to buy the best shares, but much less attention is paid to deciding when to sell. Yet everyone knows that selling is all that puts profits in your pocket.

Everyone acknowledges that paper profits scarcely matter. You cannot spend them. The profits that count are the profits you take, the cash you make, unlock, and free for spending. That is what successful investment is about, money in the bank, not profits on pieces of paper, profits that might not be there tomorrow if the stock market should crash.

Yet while investors recognise the fickle nature of paper profits, all too many forget the reality. They are reluctant to realise profits. They nurse the dream that, once made, they will be there when they need them, this year, next year, sometime . . . Maybe never?

> A simple Stop Loss system which involves selling when a price falls a pre-determined amount – say 10% or 20% – can reduce risk considerably.

Selling is the crucial second half of successful investment. Deciding when to sell is difficult. It is easy to put it off, imagining that it will all work out in the long run. In the long run, we are all dead. If you can postpone a decision to sell that long, congratulations. Perhaps that is the most successful investment of all, one that outlasts your need for it.

Most people play the share game to make money. In the simplest of terms, when the talk is of a fall ahead in share prices, or in the price of a particular share, it must make sense to consider selling. No matter that the market will almost certainly rise again later (the share might not, of course). Sell before the fall gains too much momentum, and you will have the cash to buy back in again after the fall has taken place. By acting early, you can buy a bigger stake in the action when prices are down. You will have raised your potential for profit.

There is nothing clever about it. Elementary stuff. So long as you cover your dealing expenses, it must make sense.

Relatively few people do it. They hold on and hope for an early recovery. If they just wait long enough, everything will come right, they dream. After all, that is what the City says all of the time – long term investment is the way to make money. The message comes across so loud and clear that it is easy to forget that the City has a vested interest in telling people to hold on. Big institutional investors are too heavily committed to sell. There may – literally – not be enough buyers to take the shares they want to sell. And institutional sellers would move prices so sharply against themselves that they would end up with massive losses, and would push prices down and down in a panic sell-off spiral. No big investor wants that to happen, and no fund manager will want to see investors selling his investment trust or unit trust, cutting his bonuses along the way.

> If they just wait long enough, everything will come right, they dream.

The Stop Loss System

Investors are often reluctant to take profits and sell winning shares. They fall in love with them on the way up. Should they start to slide, it is hard to accept that the glory days are over, that there will not be a return to form soon. It feels more comfortable to stay with a friend which has done you proud.

Above all, individual investors are reluctant to sell because it means making a decision. That is difficult. Inertia is a powerful force. Far easier to wait and see, then to wait a little longer. Then to hope it will get better again. If you sell too soon, you will curse your mistake, hanker after the profits you might have made by doing nothing and holding on. If the price falls, and all you lose is profit, that never seems so bad. It could always come right again, given time.

The Stop Loss system solves many of these problems. It is not perfect. No investment formula ever is. But it works more effectively than any system I have come across in 35 years as a financial journalist and investor.

It may feel wrong to substitute some form of automatic rule for your investment judgement, but the great merit of the Stop Loss system is that it removes individual judgement from the formula. It is dispassionate. The idea of selling on a fall of 10% or 20% takes away the subjective factors which go into share picking. It eliminates the emotion. It stops you from persuading yourself that this time, things are different, and if you hold on, this one really will come right.

It Is Right More Often Than Not

Sometimes it does come right, and the system is wrong. I have used the Stop Loss for more than 30 years. Experience tells me that it is right far more often than it is wrong, especially when there is no clear general market trend. In a bull market, when shares all around are rising, it can prompt you to sell too soon, no matter how carefully you try to set the system. In the long run, though, when things inevitably start to go wrong, it pays off.

A share is not forever. Shares are for buying and selling.

In a way, the name is misleading. The Stop Loss system is a classic way of prompting investors to follow the common sense rule – cut losses quickly, let your profits run. It makes you minimise losses.

More than that, though, it can play an important part in helping maximise profits. No-one sells at the top, except by luck. Using a Stop Loss means you never sell at the very top, but you do improve your chances of selling winners close to the top.

Crucially, that releases money for re-investment, invaluable in a rising market. It forces you to make decisions, forces you to think about what you are really doing in the great share game.

A share is not forever. Shares are for buying and selling. This book is not aimed at professional investors with millions to manage. It is intended to help private investors who want to make money, people with anything from £500 to £50,000, money they can afford to risk, but would not want to lose. Or perhaps it will appeal to those with £100,000, or more, who are prepared to risk some portion of it in the hope of getting an above-average return.

These are the kind of people who have been reading the share tipping column I re-started in the Daily Mail in the autumn of 1992, convinced there was investment money to be made when we were forced out of the European Exchange Rate Mechanism. I had given up my previous share tipping column in 1986, a year ahead of the Crash, worried that prices were getting overheated.

In the autumn of 1992, I also published a book entitled 'How To Profit From The Coming Share Boom' (Scope International). I did not promise an immediate boom, but was convinced there would be one in the nineties. Since then, the market has soared.

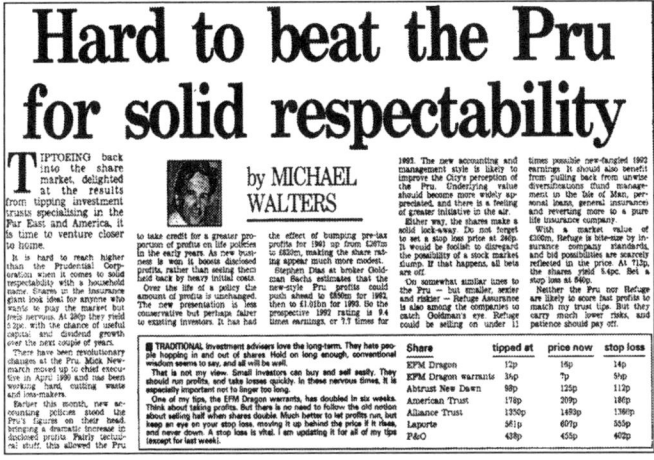

The start of the share tipping column in the *Daily Mail*.
Daily Mail, 16 November 1992

Anyone who moved into the market in the year after my book appeared should have done very well. There was no special formula, just a dash of common sense which helped me get the timing right. Clearly there are times to be in the stock market, when opportunities are good. And there are times when uncertainty is such that it is best to stay away. Shares are for buying and for selling, and there is little point in having your money at risk in them when times are tricky.

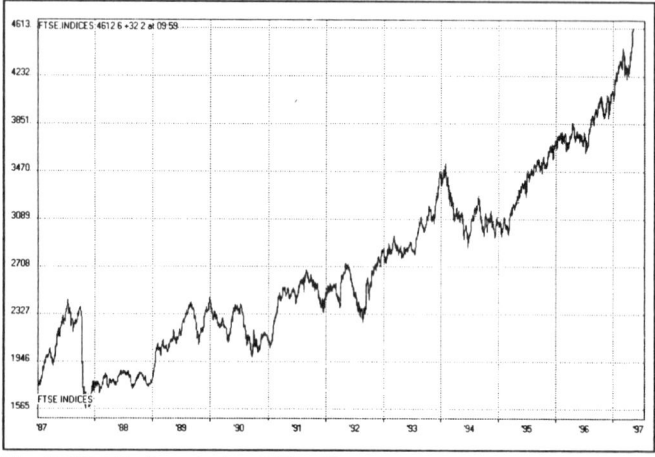

The FTSE 100 share index 1987-1997
Source: Updata Investment

Though I have been highly selective, and have sometimes not tipped a share for several weeks, each year in my *Daily Mail* column I have recommended shares which have doubled in a matter of months. Several have gone up three, four, five times or more inside 18 months before I have advised taking profits. With few exceptions, none of my tips have lost more than 20%. Most of the losers have lost 10% or less. All of my tips have been accompanied by a Stop Loss price, updated every four or five weeks, telling readers when to sell.

A few tips were sold too soon. A few rose very strongly after I advised taking profits, or cutting a small loss. But no-one who followed my advice would have sustained any serious loss. And there have been many marvellous profits. All of my

> With few exceptions, none of my tips have lost more than 20%.

examples use the price at which I have advised selling, either specifically, or through the Stop Loss. So if you were smarter at selling than I was, or updated your Stop Loss more quickly than I was able to in print, you might have done rather better.

This bout of boasting is here to illustrate a point. It has been possible to buy and sell, to deal actively in and out of the market, and to make very handsome profits, even if you did nothing more than follow advice from your newspaper.

Thanks to the Stop Loss formula in my column, the risks have been limited. This has enabled me to recommend several stocks which others might consider high risk – soaraway high technology, or biotechnology shares, for instance.

£1,000 To £120,000: Available To You

Safeguarded by a Stop Loss system, the tips have generated high returns with relatively modest risk. Readers could have gone from a stock which doubled (Standard Chartered Bank, bought November 1992 at 570p, sold February 1993 at 1190p) into a stock which trebled (Utility Cable, bought November 1993 at 6p, sold June, 1994 at 30p), and another which quadrupled

(Unipalm, bought March 1995 at 118p, sold October, 1995 at 500p) to another which quintupled (BTG, bought at 113p, October 1995, still held at 650p in the spring of 1997), all inside five years.

That doubling, trebling, quadrupling and quintupling process would have taken an initial investment of £1,000 to £120,000, all on ideas available in public for all to see, in a newspaper which sells more than two million copies a day.

Not bad. But a fairy tale. To achieve such a staggering result would have meant picking several of my biggest winners, and ignoring the more pedestrian performers and those which actually lost money. The figures, though, are real. I did recommend the shares I list, and the Stop Loss system prompted me to suggest selling at the prices I have reported. In truth, my £1,000 to £120,000 example understates what would have happened using the actual published figures, as anyone who follows the example through will see. The profit on this real, but improbable example, would have been much bigger.

Perhaps I ought not to report it, but it is hard to resist. As a way of distorting reality to achieve an unrealistically flattering performance, let me promise you, it comes nowhere near matching the tricks some of the big City houses pull to present their performances in a better light.

Perhaps, though, it is worth reporting because, from time to time, I do come across private investors who have made breath-taking profits from small beginnings. Happily, several *Daily Mail* readers have contacted me to say how well they have done from following my column. Then there is my stockbroker pal who told me he had made £200,000 from his own share trading when we first lunched a couple of years back, and who spent a more recent lunch wondering how he could reduce the capital gains tax on his new £4m fortune. You can dream. Sometimes it does come true. And when someone tells you how much money you would have made in theory by putting £1,000 into the stock market average 30 years ago and leaving it sound asleep, untouched by human hand, remember what you might have made in theory by following the *Daily Mail*, using a Stop Loss system. Each year, I think I can never be so lucky and tip so well again. It cannot last. And I promise myself that, if I think the market is getting too dangerous, I will simply stop writing share recommendations.

The real point, though, of reporting this is to illustrate that it is possible to generate high returns by using a Stop Loss system to contain risks. The Stop Loss helps, and it does more than simply limiting losses and protecting profits. By prompting you to sell from time to time, it helps you keep your money working. You take your profits, look for a new target, and reinvest. Sometimes simply sitting too long with a winner can be a mistake. You might do better switching from one which has, say, trebled to another which might double. That first big gain in a new stock – from one to two – may be easier than waiting for a winner to double from three to six. Think about the money involved. If you found a share which has gone from 10p to 30p, it needs a leap to 60p to double your money. In cash terms, that might mean your £1,000 has gone to £3,000. It might be easier to put your £3,000 in another 10p stock, hoping it will rise by 10p to 20p, than by hanging on hoping for your first 10p stock to rise another 30p. It can be done if you are ready to work at investing, ready to play the game, and to take advantage of the fact that shares can rise and fall sharply over quite short periods.

Successful active investment can make a real difference. If you have between £500 and £50,000 to invest, matching market performance over the long term is nice, but will hardly change your life. At that level, a 10% or even a 20% gain is welcome, but hardly crucial. Some investors will think it better to live a little, limit the downside by using a Stop Loss, and go for the higher returns which could make a real difference. Double your money in three or four years, and perhaps then you have enough to think seriously about longer term investment policies, and substituting inertia for active investment.

There are no promises, no guarantees, in this book, just the belief that active investment can pay for the private shareholder. Picking the right share is half the story. Deciding when to sell it, being brave enough to take the decision, is the other half. The Stop Loss system can help make that difficult move so much easier.

This is a book about selling shares. That does not mean it is all gloom and doom, with the emphasis on the dangers and the downside. A sensible, logical approach to selling massively reduces the risks of investing. Limiting the down-side enhances the upside. It helps introduce a much broader choice for active investors, opening up opportunities in potential high-flying companies which might otherwise appear too risky.

The Stop Loss system is not just about stopping losses. It is also about making the most of opportunities, about encouraging active investment.

Eastern deals promise a great future for Verity

INVESTMENT EXTRA

By **MICHAEL WALTERS**

WHAT a worrisome week it has been. Wall Street wobbled, London stuttered, but held pretty firm. And headlines about £20bn stock market losses made it all look much worse than it really was.

It seems to happen every year around this time. The gloomsters get into gear, stock markets slip and slide and then go to sleep for a spell. And, each year, anyone with the nerve to buy is making good money by the autumn.

This time, it might be different. Interest rates are edging higher in the US, and a Labour Government looks likely to raise them here. We could have a sticky spell — though, given the strength of the economy here and in the US, the bull run may be far from over.

Sadly, there can be no guarantees. One day, the slump will come. So keep watching and keep counting your share-dealing profits.

Never get shaken out of decent shares by predictions of a setback from pundits who never dirty their hands by selecting individual shares themselves. Share prices convey the message that matters. When they start to fall, that is what counts. Keep a stop-loss level alive to determine how much risk you will take before you switch into cash.

Do not consider the stop-loss simply as a negative force, protecting you from losses and sheltering profits. It also helps to promote an active portfolio. A week ago, it suggested selling Blacks Leisure after they had more than doubled in less than a year. Blacks could well go better — indeed, the shares have already staged some recovery — but sellers have released funds for new investment. Blacks might not double again in the year ahead, but active investors might hope to reinvest in something that will.

Once again, the portfolio continues to score useful gains. It was particularly pleasing to see Verity Group shrug off negative comment, and rise nicely on news of an agreement with Samsung, Korea's largest electronics company. Samsung will make loudspeakers using the revolutionary flat-panel loudspeaker technology developed by Verity subsidiary NXT.

This goes beyond the earlier deal with Japanese giant NEC, which covered applications in laptop computers. Samsung will use NXT technology in personal computers, multi-media and audio and video products.

Other players look sure to follow, especially now that a couple of the biggest names in the business have effectively endorsed the system.

Share	Date	Price tipped	Price now	Stop-Loss	Action
Hay & Robertson	Oct 2, 95	36p	145p	125p	hold
BTG	Nov 20, 95	113p	630p	480p	rsl
Biocompatibles	Aug 10, 96	352p	1250p	1050p	rsl
Persona	Aug 17, 96	323p	343½p	303p	hold
FirstBus	Sep 28, 96	170½p	231p	200p	rsl
Zeneca	Oct 5, 96	1665p	1883p	1710p	rsl
Tepnel	Oct 12, 96	37½p	72½p	54p	rsl
Gander	Nov 2, 96	12½p	14¾p	12¾p	rsl
American Port	Nov 9, 96	117½p	167½p	140p	rsl
National Parking	Dec 21, 96	470p	580p	470p	hold
English National	Feb 8, 97	209p	208p	150p	hold
Verity	Feb 22, 97	41¾p	48¼p	36p	rsl
Shield Diagnostic	Feb 22, 97	529½p	602½p	480p	hold
Ennstone	Mar 8, 97	3p	3¼p	1½p	hold
Innovative Tech	Mar 15, 97	352½p	330p	270p	hold
Caldwell	Mar 22, 97	57p	64p	46p	hold
Regalian	Ap 5, 87	41½p	43½p	33p	hold

(rsl means raise stop-loss)

Chris Radmore at house broker Peel Hunt cautions that it will be 1998-99 before substantial revenue starts flowing to Verity, but reckons the potential market is enormous. It runs into tens of billions of pounds and stretches way beyond conventional speakers to anything from electronic products to cars, planes, buildings and much more.

Verity's market value of £154m at 54¾p may look demanding for a company that is making little money — but the potential is massive.

Similar notions apply to Biocompatibles, which has quadrupled from 352p to 1420p in the eight months since it was tipped. The news gets better and better. The US Food & Drug Administration has granted permission to market the Proclear Compatibles monthly replaceable soft contact lens in the US. This uses Biocompatibles technology to give the lens greater resistance to drying out and to becoming clogged with deposits from the eye.

Biocompatibles should now be able to attract a powerful US marketing partner quickly on good terms. The company has spent £7.4m buying Surfacine, an anti-bacterial coating technology, to enhance its own techniques. There should be a steady flow of new agreements, with hopes of securing Johnson & Johnson to market Biocompatible stents (little metal devices that hold blood vessels open), and progress towards an anti-fouling marine paint.

Pre-tax losses were £18.5m for 1996, but pre-tax profits could hit £20m for 1998, then really start to rocket. Brokers still project a share price of 1600p — and higher.

Spring 1997: the share tipping column in the *Daily Mail*
Daily Mail, 12 April 1997

◆◆◆

Improving Performance

Never mind the nail-biting about the trade deficit, European Monetary Union, the Chancellor versus the Governor of the Bank of England, the accounting treatment of goodwill, and the appropriate level of discounted cash flow. The stock market is fun.

You can take it just as seriously as you choose. If much of it appears gobbledegook to you, good enough. Ignore it. You may well be right, in the end. Unless you become too deeply committed, you can treat share investment as a great and glorious game, played on just as many levels as you wish. The trade deficit, EMU, and all of that stuff do play some part, but you can perfectly well spot an exciting share and enjoy the ride without paying the slightest attention to economic affairs. They might impinge on your investment at some stage. If they go badly awry, they might bring the whole market crashing down, and your shares with it. But they might not.

There are other books which discuss whether or not you should play the stock market, and how you might select winning shares. I have written several of them. Hopefully, you are reading this book because you are already in the share game. So this is not about the basics – except for one. It would be totally irresponsible of me not to emphasise that you should not be in the stock market unless you are using money you can afford to lose.

Active Share Traders Can Do It . . .

Share trading is dangerous. Over the long term, the stock market has risen strongly, and long term investment in equities has provided far superior returns to other forms of investment. Most of us, though, cannot wait for the long term. We want more, and we want it now – or relatively soon.

Active share traders can do it. The rewards from playing a rising stock market can be quite startling. In 1996, the market rose by 11%. The best performing share was Blacks Leisure, which ran a chain of sports and leisure wear shops. It gained 590%, well outstripping the rest. Jarvis, a construction company, gained 526%. Ferrum, an engineering business, rocketed from 1p to 7p. There was a small oil company called Cairn Energy, up 268%. And a clutch of football clubs – Celtic (which few investors would have bought), and two of the best-known and most widely owned, Manchester United (up 229%), and Caspian (the company

> Most of us cannot wait for the long term. We want more, and we want it now – or relatively soon.

which bought Leeds United), up 323%. And there was a housebuilder, Fairbriar, up 225%.

Many of these winners attracted abundant publicity during the year, and many small investors bought them and made handsome gains.

Sadly, many small investors would have been in some of the bottom ten. Club Partners, which owns golf clubs, fell 92%. Lionheart, a tip sheet favourite which made bathroom fittings, lost 89%. Omnimedia was hit by poor sales of CD ROM discs, and lost 80%. Diagnostic research company Electrophoretics touched 200p and ended the year at 38½p.

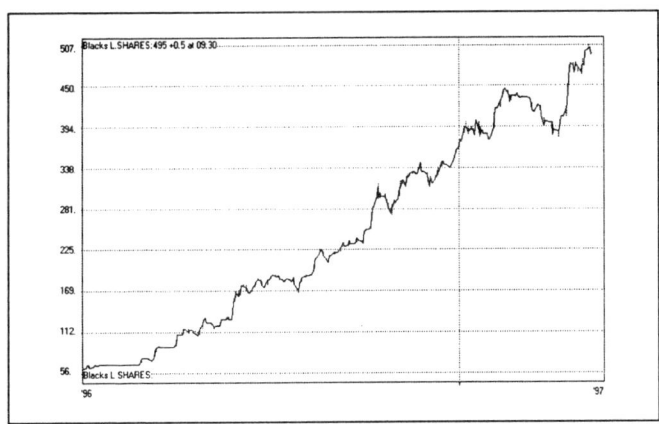

Blacks Leisure 1996-1997
Source: Updata Investment

In my Investment Extra column which appeared most weeks in the *Daily Mail*, I made 19 recommendations. By the end of 1996, all but two had been sold, 12 at a profit, three at a loss, and two at break-even.

Two big winners carried over from the previous year, with BTG up 275% and Hay & Robertson up 268%, both inside fifteen months at the end of 1996. Tepnel Life Sciences was sold during the year. In at 15p, it was Stop Lossed out at 60p, after touching 82p. Other big winners sold in that year included Carpetright, up from 228p to 530p after touching 644p, Shield Diagnostics, in at 67p and out at 140p, and Regalian, in at 19p and out at 37½p.

In 1995, I made 25 recommendations, and Stop Lossed two out at modest losses. Two others were showing small losses at the year-end, but everything else was up. Six tips had doubled, or better, in a few months. Star performer was Internet access provider Unipalm, tipped at 118p and taken over at a price which eventually hit a freak 890p thanks to a surge in the price of the American bidder. I suggested selling, though, at 500p and 440p.

More thrills than spills on the merry-go-round

INVESTMENT EXTRA

By MICHAEL WALTERS

OWN-UP time. Fingers crossed, after a very good year in 1995 when I picked six stocks which doubled or better within months — headlined by a sevenfold leap in internet service provider Unipalm — it worked out pretty well in 1996.

There was no monster here to rival Unipalm, and there were more losers than I like to admit. On the stop-loss system, there was nothing too damaging.

Once again, there were some big winners. At the turn of the year, my list features 11 recommendations. By the end of 1996, all but two had been sold, 12 at a profit, three at a loss, and two at break-even. Two losers were recovered when the stop-loss took them out — Chiroscience down 10pc and CeilSs 18pc lower.

Two big winners from 1996 are still running. I should feel a little bitter at profits unless there is a general market setback. At one stage, BTG was up more than fourfold. At 424p, it is up more than threefold on the price of 113p, allowing for a five-for-one split. Hay & Robertson is up from 36p to 133½p, a rise of 268pc. Both might still have been achieved inside 15 months.

BTG helps develop and exploit inventions, with a portfolio packed with potential in anything from new drugs to electronic tags. Crucial to shorter-term performance is the Torotrak infinitely variable transmission system. That could develop into a motor industry standard in the next century. If it does — nothing is certain yet — BTG shares still have a long way to go.

Lance Yates is building Hay & Robertson fast into a significant leisurewear company, boosted by a deal to exploit gear linked to Chelsea football coach Ruud Gullit. The shares are looking some way ahead, but the future is bright.

Last year's other big winner was tiny Tepnel Life Sciences. Recommended at 8p the equivalent to 15p, it soared to 88p before. I suggested preserving profits at 60p. Four times your money in just over a year looked good. Recently I have been recommending gamblers to buy Tepnel again at lower levels.

Other big winners which were sold in 1996 included Carpetright, in at 222p in September 1994, out at 530p (after 644p) in July 1996. Shield Diagnostics came in at 67p in August 1995, and out at 140p in July 1996. And property group Raglan, in at 19p in July 1995, went out at 37½p just over a year later.

As the year unfolded, there were 20 winners and five losers on the stop-loss system. Five were sold at a profit in a matter of months, led by English National Investment. In at 48p in February, it topped 100p before being stop-lossed out at 75p in October.

There were six losers, with the worst being tiny Thomas Potts, down from 14p to 4p. A major acquisition fell through late in the day. There are hopes of another deal soon. That, apart, the other losers were modest.

Ten of this year's tips are still running. The table below updates their stop-loss levels. Two have seen more than doubled, with Blacks Leisure up from 186p in June to 374p, and Biocompatibles up from the equivalent of 352p in August to 905p.

Stick with them both. Blacks had a cracking Christmas. Top retail analyst Nick Bubb at MeesPierson is raising his profit forecasts for this year yet again. Biocompatibles, from 122m? The chill winter is helping the ski-wear and more rugged leisurewear sales.

Mover of the moment is American Pulp Services, up sharply in as the strength of sterling has reduced the value of dollar profits. Brokers and big investors are about to visit the company's east-coast facilities, and broker Greig Middleton is preparing a circular which will forecast profits of £6.6m for 1996 and £9m for 1997.

The company has already made one extremely cheap acquisition, and further corporate activity could be on the horizon.

SHARE	DATE	PRICE THEN	PRICE NOW	STOP LOSS	ACTION
Hay & Robertson	Oct 2	36p	133½p	108p	ra
BTG	Nov 20	113p	424p	349p	ra
Blacks Leisure	Jun 10	352p	905p	790p	ra
Biocompatibles	Aug 10	352p	905p	790p	ra
FirstBus	Aug 28	170½p	203½p	178p	ra
Zeneca	Oct 5	1665p	1648½p	1485p	ra
Tepnel	Oct 5	325p	267½p	222p	ra
DCS	Oct 28	124½p	114½p	104½p	ra
Gaunder	Nov 9	117½p	104½p	100½p	ra
American Port	Nov 7	65p	58p	58p	hold
Whitney	Dec 7				

(ra) means raise stop loss

The Investment Extra Column
Daily Mail, 4 January 1997

The Optimistic Investor

So it is possible to make a killing in the share jungle. But it is also possible to get it wrong, to get killed. In 1996, not too many quoted companies went bust, wiping out every penny shareholders had invested in them. A few did. And those in the Top Ten losers list inflicted massive losses on investors who did nothing, but simply held on and hoped that something would turn up to make their investment work in the longer run.

Never forget the dangers. It suits the investment community to wear a happy face, to take a positive view. Stockbrokers produce vast volumes of research for big clients. Relatively few suggest selling. Buy notes are more popular. No matter how we try to eliminate emotions most investors are optimists at heart. We want to buy, want to see prices rising, even though it is possible to make big money by anticipating problems, and selling in expectation of a fall.

> No matter how we try, most investors are optimists at heart.

The risk in share investment is generally understated. Relatively few fund managers survive from the early seventies, when the FT Index slumped from over 500 to 146. Shares in some of our biggest companies plunged into the penny stock league. There are more City folk who lived through the Crash of '87. A hurricane hit the South of England, sending chimneys crashing through roofs, and trees tumbling onto cars. It made for a surreal mood in the City as the Financial Times Index lost 500 points in two trading sessions, spooked by a fall on Wall Street. Shares galore lost a quarter of their value inside a week.

Such a dramatic setback might never happen again, although markets have become much more volatile. Through the mid-nineties, the mood has been such to suggest that any sharpish setback presents a buying opportunity. Underlying economic fundamentals have been improving in the USA and the UK, inflation has been in check, interest rates have been subdued, and all has looked fairly good.

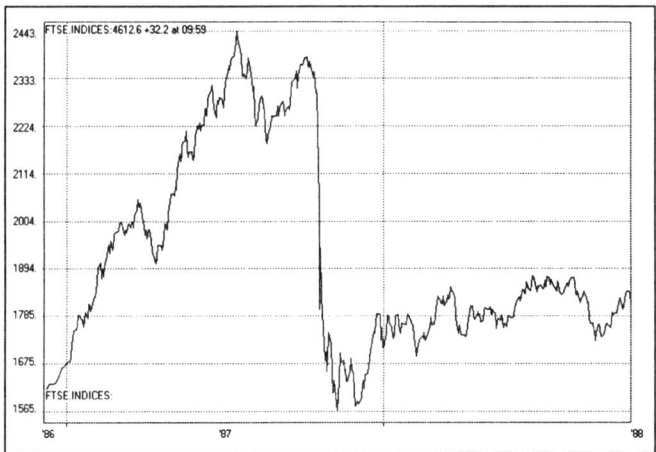

The crash of '87
Source: Updata Investment

Even though a setback was not entirely unexpected, the Crash of '87 came as a shock when it happened. It illustrates the dangers of share investment, then and now. Just because the market did not lose 500 points last week, or fall by a quarter, does not mean that the risk was not present. It was. It is. If you were holding shares, you got away with it. Maybe next week . . .

Any share setback could create a buying opportunity. But not necessarily at once. After the Crash of '87, the market dithered nervously. There was an economic recession in the early nineties, and it was not until the autumn of 1992 that the market really began to get into its stride again.

Headline news . . . the crash of '87.
Daily Mail, 20 October 1987

After we were pushed out of the European Exchange Rate Mechanism in September 1992, and the way was clear for a reduction in interest rates which would allow our economy to start moving forward, it became apparent that there was good money to be made in the share market. In my book 'How To Profit From The Coming Share Boom' (Scope International), which was actually written in the spring of 1992 and published in the autumn, just ahead of our exit from the ERM, I suggested 'the boom is ahead, not behind us. The instant the economic scene allows it, the big money will come pouring back, generating profits for all.' The book was 'designed to help you cash in on the opportunity of the decade.'

As it turned out, that proved remarkably well timed. It demonstrates that anyone with any common sense could see what would happen. It always seems to happen, boom follows slump, and slump follows boom. Share prices rise, share prices fall.

It has always been so. While it would be wonderful to think that our economic leaders have grown smart enough to ensure eternal economic prosperity, steady growth and modest inflation, as we move towards the Millennium, it is almost certainly too good to be true. Sooner or later, something will go wrong. Perhaps inflation will get out of hand and interest rates will be forced higher, reining industry back sharply. Or perhaps it will be trouble in Tokyo, with a resurgence of the Yen, a reversal of the flood of Japanese money into America, and a consequent slump in US bond and share prices which upsets us all.

Act For Yourself

Whatever the reason, we are likely to suffer a stock market setback sooner or later. Perhaps it will be different next time. Perhaps the massed chorus of vested interests will prevail. Perhaps so many people will have come to accept the idea that, long term, the only way for the stock market is up and so relatively few will sell. The market will suffer a brief blip, then go bounding on up. No need to worry about what happens.

If that is what you believe, this book is not for you. This book is for those who like to think for themselves, to act for themselves. This book is for those who are ready to throw off inertia and indecision, and to try to sell high and buy low.

> This book is for those who like to think for themselves, to act for themselves. This book is for those who are ready to throw off inertia and indecision, and to try to sell high and buy low.

It must make sense. Ahead of the '87 Crash, ICI (before the demerger into ICI and Zeneca) was a revered blue-chip, and was riding high. On Friday October 16, 1987, immediately before the Crash, it fell 12p to 1,583p. Taking a date almost at random, it was 1,045p on February 16, 1988, just four months later. In those four months, it had lost more than 500p a share, over a third of its value.

You could not have saved all of that loss by selling as soon as trouble hit. But you could have saved a great chunk of it. There was no need to sit and simply watch your capital crumble. On Wednesday, October 21, the market bounced, retrieving 142 points. ICI closed at 1,305p. It was down 278p from the price a few days earlier, just ahead of the Crash. Bad news. Crucially, though, it was still 260p above the price it fell to by

February 16, a few months later. Even selling after the Crash, you would have saved much of the pain. If you had been operating a Stop Loss system before the Crash, building in a promise to sell on a 20% fall, your selling target would have been 1,267p. Despite the dramatic fall in share prices, you would have been able to meet it. And selling then would have paid off.

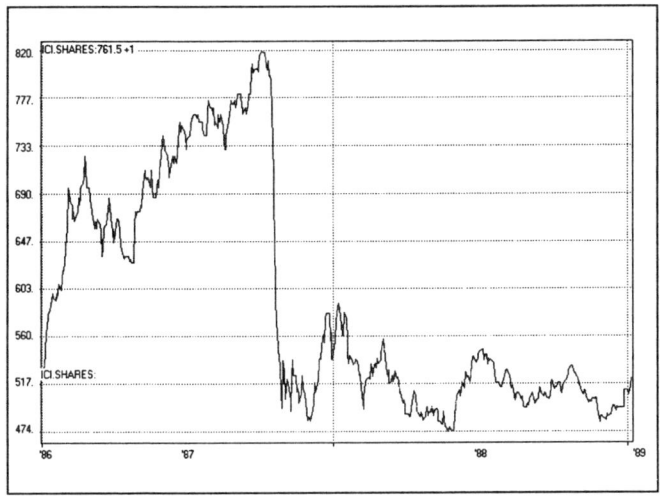

ICI: 1986-89
Source: Updata Investment

ICI did fall more than some, but it was not too untypical. Look at Great Universal Stores. It was 1,418p on October 16, and 1,040p on February 16. Sears went from 170p to 122p, Thorn EMI from 717p to 553p, GEC from 232p to 151p, Marks & Spencer from 251p to 172p, and so on.

There are examples galore, some much more dramatic, especially among second and third line companies. A few shares actually rose over the period. But not many. Like the other examples, ICI was a substantial company. No matter what short term trading problems it might encounter, the probability was that it would recover. And, as many pointed out at the time, nothing much had changed within the business over that period. The company you bought into in February 1988 was substantially the same company as you bought a share in four months early. All that had changed was the stock market rating, the share price.

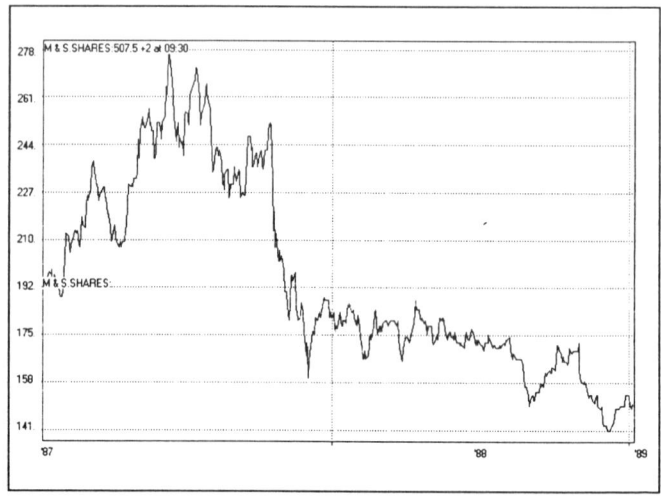

Marks & Spencer 1987-89
Source: Updata Investment

Why, though, sit tight in the shares when the whole mood of the market had changed, when the risks of a setback in the price were clear to see in the second half of October 1987? Suddenly the risk profile of share investment had changed. Why sit with the extra risk?

It was possible to sell after the Crash, and save money. Returning to the examples above, on Wednesday October 21, immediately after the Crash, GUS shares were 1,195p, Sears were 136p, Thorn EMI 605p, GEC 201p, Marks & Spencer 220p. All were significantly lower by February, and some suffered quite heavy extra losses. The examples are chosen because they represent well-known, widely-held investments, not because they support my selling argument particularly – though they do.

Selling In A Crisis

In truth, anyone who was running a system which suggested they sell on a 10% fall might have been able to scramble out without too much damage. On Monday, October 19, the second day of the two-day Crash, the index slumped 249.6 points. If you had taken fright at the similar slump on the previous trading day, the Friday, perhaps you would have been in there, selling into the fall on Monday. It would have paid off. On the Monday, ICI fell 184p to 1,399p. GUS lost 80p to 1,338p, Sears 18½p to 151½p, Thorn EMI 59p to 658p, GEC 33p to 199p, and Marks & Spencer 29p to 222p.

Think about it. Amid the chaos, you might not actually have been able to sell. Brokers and market-makers were not answering their phones for most of the day, knowing they were facing a flood of sell orders. But if you did move quickly and decisively, with a pre-planned selling system in mind, you might have been lucky. The prices above are taken from the closing list on a day when everything was falling. You might have been able to scramble out above the closing price, with luck.

Do not be misled. There are no guarantees. But when people start attacking those who sell on panicky days, they tend to be the chaps who never got round to doing anything themselves. Or perhaps the kind of market commentators who have never held a share in their life, and who have no idea about the way things really work. They can afford to adopt a patronising tone of lofty detachment. A crash matters not a jot to them. They can always be right, with hindsight.

Consider, too, the nature of the shares in my examples. Pretty blue chip, every one of them. No speculative high flyers there, nothing liable to fall out of bed at the first tremor. Many investors might have considered they were the sort of stocks they could hold for ever, companies which might come close to winning the Buffett seal of approval.

Yet when the crunch came in October 1987, they proved every bit as vulnerable as all the rest. There had been nothing much to insulate them from the upset, after all. The Crash really spared no-one, spreading across the whole market with only rare exceptions.

Take a few of the racier stocks, pretty much at random. See how they fared. Bodycote fell from 385p ahead of the Crash to 345p on the Wednesday immediately after. Four months later, in mid-February, it was 232p. Using the same dates throughout, try other examples. Albert Fisher went from 238p to 192p, then 101p, Helene from 76p to 61p to 39p, Polly Peck from 418p to 319p, then 299p, high-flyer Thomas Robinson from 644p to 517p to 420p. At that stage, Richard Branson had brought Virgin to market. It moved from 156p to 127p to 130p. Body Shop proved a real maverick. At 860p before the crash, it fell sharply, and recovered 200p to 825p by the Wednesday after. Four months later, it was actually higher, at 915p.

> By and large, the blue chips offered no great protection to the average investor.

Look at the property sector, where it was quite clear there would be problems after the initial crash, and where everyone should have sold. One of the leaders, British Land, fell from 320p before the Crash to 250p immediately after, then rebounded to 274p in February (it touched 110p in 1992). Urban residential developer Regalian was 283p before the Crash, 233p immediately after, and 155p four months later (at one stage later, it went under 3p).

On the whole, using a Stop Loss to scramble out of anything in the Crash would have saved money. As months went by, the smallest and weakest of the speculative stocks did fare worst. But, by and large, the blue chips offered no great protection to the average investor. The notion that they were safer than the average shares proved false.

The Way To Improve Performance

Unless you are in some sort of Tracker fund, mimicking the share index, no individuals buy and sell the whole market. Private investors are much more concerned with day to day changes in individual shares. And when prices fall, they are telling you something. They are suggesting that, perhaps, you have got it wrong. The share you expected to rise is falling. Perhaps someone knows better than you. Whether they do or not, if sufficient people are selling to push the price down, it may be that sufficient people will carry on selling, pushing the price still lower.

In such circumstances, it looks a matter of simple prudence to heed the message, and to sell. Why risk staying in when the mood has changed, when the money you have at stake is dribbling away? Far better to shift into cash, and move back in when the mood is steadier.

That, of course, is the way not simply to cut risks, but to improve performance. It would be nice to finesse it, to sell at the top, sit with cash, then buy back in at the bottom. No-one manages to do that, except by sheer good fortune. But even if you sell after a 10% or 20% fall, sit with the cash, and buy back after a 10% rise from the bottom, you will do better than the manager who has simply sat tight, weathering the storm. And in doing so, you have removed the risk that a sharp setback might turn into something really nasty. The institutional fund manager has been sitting with that risk, whether he likes it or not.

"The big boys . . . most things are slanted their way."

As a private investor, you can move in and out of the market reasonably freely. That gives you a major advantage over the big boys. Most things in the City are slanted their way. They are kept up to date with company progress regularly,

> As a private investor, you can move in and out of the market reasonably freely. That gives you a major advantage over the big boys.

often consulted before any big deal, usually notified by the company or the company's brokers of any change in profit expectations. In theory, they are not allowed to act on such information. They are effectively made insiders, and cannot deal. In practice, the system leaks around the edges. A little stock will always be bought or sold, reflecting what is really happening. Sometimes, a lot of stock will move.

Happily, the institutions are rarely in a position to shift too much stock. Their holdings are simply too big. When they want to buy, companies sometimes supply them by issuing new stock in a deal, and getting the institutions to take it in a placing, or as underwriters. Or the company's broker can informally put together a group of sellers to satisfy the would-be buyer.

Selling is trickier. In good times, it might be possible to find other institutional buyers to take stock. When the market is going nowhere, and especially when it is going down, it becomes impossible to sell large lines. The market-makers will only take quite modest amounts before marking prices down. And the seller does not want to see prices marked down. That will make the performance of his fund look bad. He has to answer to directors and to trustees. So long as he can keep somewhere near the middle of the pack, only doing badly when everyone else is, there will not be too much of a problem. But if a fund manager should try to shift a big line of stock and see the price marked down against him, cutting the value of the shares he has not managed to shift, that is bad news. There will be questions from directors, from trustees, league table positions to worry about, and so on.

Big fund managers are poor sellers. They find it difficult. Many unit trust and investment trust managers even suggest it is their duty to stay invested, whatever the market. That is what their investors pay them for, they say. Perhaps. Given the choice, most investors would probably say they are choosing fund managers to manage their investments to make money, rather than to lie doggo in a crisis. No wonder the City convention is to tell the world not to panic in any crash. If small investors wade in and start selling, they will push prices down, and undermine the value of the holdings the big boys cannot possibly sell. So they look bad.

The sensible private individual can sell much more easily. If the going looks sticky, private investors can get out, though second and third line stocks can be tricky at times. The secret is not to become over-committed to any one stock. When you buy in, always keep getting out in mind. Always get your broker to check the size of the market with the market-maker. What is listed as the 'normal market size' is usually misleading, and understates true liquidity. Get your broker to see how many market-makers there are – the more, the merrier – and what volume of stock they will normally trade at the quoted price. If you go over the usual trade volume, be careful. It could be difficult to sell when you wish, especially since market-makers can widen the spread between buying and selling prices, and cut their dealing volumes when the going gets hard.

> The secret is not to become over-committed to any one stock.

The freedom to switch easily into cash, to cut and run whenever the going gets dangerous, is an invaluable advantage to the individual investor. Use it. No good sitting there worrying about your shares. Cash, or a building society account, may not be exciting. But it is safe. Never forget why you go into the stock market – to make money, and to have a little fun. Once the fun stops, there is no point in being there, no need to take on extra worry. If it looks as if your profits are slipping away, sell. If your loss in some stock is beginning to mount, sell. Unlike the boys in the City, you have no-one to answer to but yourself. And it is your money at risk. Time and again, it comes back to one of the clearest, simplest investment rules of all – if in doubt, sell out.

Filtering Out The Losers

The decision to sell shares does get tangled up in a web of emotion. Try as you may, it is impossible to stay absolutely detached from the investment process. Picking a winner is wonderful, and not just for the money it makes. It delivers a great boost to your ego. There is real satisfaction in proving that you got it right. The how and why does not matter. So long as the price has gone up, and you can sell for more than you paid, you were right. Inside, you might acknowledge sometimes that much of it was luck. There was a bid out of the blue, or a newspaper tip sent it soaring, or some completely new product or research suddenly surfaced.

It does not matter. You got it right, and that is good enough. That can make parting with it difficult. It has become an old friend. If you have held it for a while, you may have got some feel for the way the price moves. You know in advance how it will behave on good market days, and on bad.

Should it begin to fall, it is hard to imagine the good times are over. There is a temptation to think it will recover, start rising again. Any setback seems temporary. Selling would be a wrench. It is always good to be able to think you are holding a share which has done well for you, doubled, or perhaps trebled. Since you are ahead, you can afford to be patient. It is easy to pretend that any fall in the price is not costing you much, just taking back a little of the profit.

Be careful. Carry on that way, and soon all of the profit could be gone, You could be looking at a winner turned loser. Much better to sell before the slide gathers pace. Play safe.

The Crucial Rule

If anything, parting company with a loser seems worse. After all, selling a loser amounts to admitting you got it wrong. If you investigated it carefully before you bought, that comes hard. You will be tempted to hold on, persuading yourself that the market has yet to appreciate the virtues you discovered. It may only be a matter of time.

The letters, calls and conversations which have given me a glimpse into the way investors operate suggests that, all too often, they will do almost anything to give a loser a second chance. In the *Daily Mail*, I make a point of expressing buy or sell recommendations in particularly emphatic fashion. Too often, I hear from investors who are on a loser, and clutch eagerly at any comment which offers a shred of hope. The

Selling a loser amounts to admitting you got it wrong.

notion of fairness, truth, and editorial balance means you cannot simply emphasise the negative in writing a piece which says 'Sell'. Sometimes, though, it would make life a lot simpler, and prove of far greater value to readers.

Everyone knows the rule. For me, it is the most important guide of all to success with shares – CUT YOUR LOSSES, AND RUN YOUR PROFITS.

It is elementary. Yet so many investors ignore it, largely because emotion creeps in, and they cannot bring themselves to admit that they have made a mistake. Holding losers in the hope that they will come right often seems to matter more than spotting a winner. Yet one winner can make up for several losers, provided you sell the losers when the losses are small.

Cut your losses and pick the winners with stop loss system

By MICHAEL WALTERS

A Michael Walters warning.
Daily Mail, 23 October 1995

Investment experts like to claim they are doing well if they pick six winners out of ten. In a bull market, that is a very modest target.

Even picking more winners than losers is no guarantee that you will make money, of course. One total loss can wipe out the gains from four modest winners. There is little need to get caught with a total loss. Very few public companies actually go bust.

> One total loss can wipe out the gains from four modest winners.

Hardly any go bust without some signs of problems in the months before it happens. In almost every case, the price starts to fall. Watch for the warning signs – sell before the bust. By the same token, there is little need to get caught with a substantial loss. The choice is yours. You can almost always sell before the loss becomes too damaging.

If you choose to accept only a modest loss each time, one good winner will make up for it. The arithmetic is simple. Start with £5,000. Put £1,000 into each of five shares. If four prove a disappointment, sell before the loss exceeds 20% loss. The £4,000 stake money has fallen to £3,200. If the fifth share should double, the overall portfolio ends up with a value of £5,200.

Terrific. One good winner has compensated for four losers – so long as those losers have been sold at a reasonable price, before the loss has grown too great.

Better still, if you have been successful, and are playing with a reasonable amount of cash, taking your losses may well have covered any capital gains tax liability you may have on your winner. The first £6,500 of realised capital gains is tax free in 1997-98. The allowance has gradually been moving up. If you have gains over £6,500 in the tax year, you pay tax on the surplus at your top tax rate. But you can offset realised losses – the losses on shares you have sold – against the gain. So active investors who have to take a loss effectively get a hand from the tax man when they break into decent profits. Long term investors, who never take a loss, steadily build up an ever bigger capital gains liability, if they have to sell at a profit.

In the bull market which has been running from the autumn of 1993 to the spring of 1997, it would have taken a pretty inept investor to pick four losers out of five. The chances of selecting one share which has doubled, or near it, would have been good – especially since the policy of selling losers quickly would permit more adventurous stock selection.

The Warren Buffett Way

Oddly enough, I have met no-one who objects to the notion that you should sell losers quickly, and sit with winners. It is a policy which appears to meet with universal approbation. And yet . . .

And yet it does not make sense if you listen to the boys in the value investment band, those who love the idea of long term investment. I have shared the platform with one or two of them at investment conferences. Because we all deliver our own little lectures, the problem only seems to arise where there is a general all-in question session at the end. Now and then, there is a hint of confusion as some long term advocate also endorses the idea of cutting losses quickly. But there never seems time to debate just how to reconcile the idea that, if you pick a solid value investment, you should sit with it, come hell or high water. Yet the same investor often says you must be sure to cut losses before they grow too great.

This little conflict appears to me to identify the fault at the core of the long term, value investor school. Warren Buffett is brilliant, wholly exceptional. He now has the wealth and power to stick with his mistakes, and to try to make sure they come right in the end. As he is first to admit, he does make mistakes. In his admirable 'Owner's Manual' for investors in his Berkshire Hathaway company, he confesses he tried for 20 years to sort out the company's textile business before closing it. He can afford to do that. His other triumphs have given him breathing space to tolerate a loser for 20 years. Few private investors can – or should – do that. This really is an example where there is one rule for the rich, another for the poor.

The average private investor, and certainly the sort of smaller player which this book is directed at, cannot afford to have part of their limited funds tied up in a loser for long. It is folly. Like it or not, that would involve unduly high risk. And it carries significant opportunity cost. Sell the loser, and you free the cash to take the opportunity of investing in something else. Something that might make good money.

And if Warren Buffett can make mistakes, the rest of us are equally vulnerable. And how can we ever be sure that we have chosen that special value stock, the share to live with for a lifetime, one which will prosper through good times or bad?

Buffett's real strength derives from picking some big winners in the early days, establishing a good solid base of gains. Finding similar gems in the UK today, stocks to hold for a lifetime, looks difficult.

Go back a few years. Imagine where you might have looked for what Buffett calls 'The Inevitables', companies whose superior returns are predictable a long way into the future, and which can therefore be valued differently.

Fading Giants

There may not be any in the UK. Jim Slater's all-powerful financial conglomerate would inevitably have caught the eye. Slater Walker Securities stormed through the late sixties and into the seventies, only to collapse. Value investors would never have taken it seriously. There was always too much controversy to place it among the all-time survivors. But James Hanson started his stock market career among the Slater Walker satellites. As he moved through the seventies and early eighties, his Hanson Trust must have looked like a great long-term winner to many. Sadly, these days, it has demerged into a shadow of itself as the share rating declined. Lord Weinstock's great creation, the General Electric Company, is another which would have warranted serious consideration. Sadly, in the nineties, it is stuck in a mediocre groove, waiting for the kiss of life from a new management team.

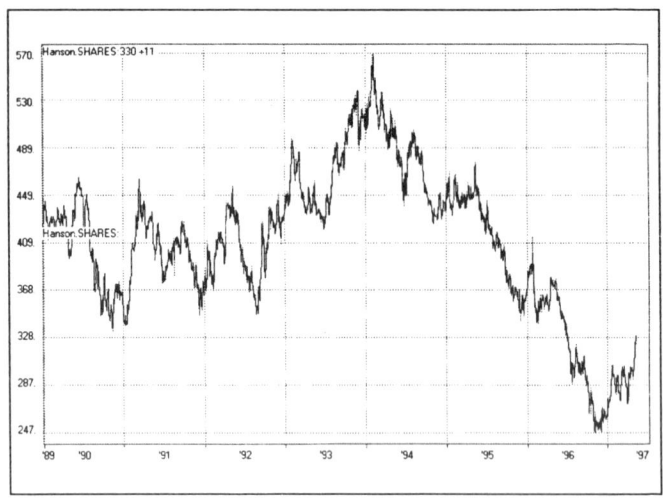

Hanson Trust 1989-97
Source: Updata Investment

Everyone loved Isaac Wolfson's Great Universal Stores once. In the nineties, the City waits to see if a different set of directors can revive it. Grand Metropolitan, owner of Burger King and Britain's answer to that recent Buffett favourite McDonald's, has stuttered along until a grand merger plan emerged. The clearing banks are better, perhaps. Few, though, will forget the day in the secondary banking collapse of the seventies when the National Westminster had to issue a statement reassuring the market that all was well. Or the billion pound losses the banks ran up on dud loans in the late eighties and early nineties.

In the late nineties, the once-mighty P & O shipping line appears to be over a crisis, but its former glory has faded. The Cunard rival vanished into Trafalgar House, the building to engineering conglomerate which all but went under a few years back. And so on, and so forth.

In Britain, it seems, the great enduring inevitables, stocks to live with for twenty years, are hard to identify. An insurance company or two, perhaps the Prudential, might fit the bill. Or that enduring monument to smooth efficiency, Marks & Spencer. They might do for me. Buffett himself did venture across the Atlantic a while back. He bought Guinness, and lost money on it. It may be that, after all, the British Buffett fans are wrestling to apply a set of disciplines which even the master recognises will not work in this country.

Investment magazines which have looked beyond Buffett and explored the idea of value investment tend to find that life has moved on. Many of the ideas attributed to the masters relate to a different, less financially sophisticated era, when it was possible to find growth shares selling at a discount to asset value. Benjamin Graham, wrote 'The Intelligent Investor', which is often described as the best book on investing. He died in 1976, and despite the eminent intelligence in his approach, the stock market has moved on – certainly for the small investor. The whole book barely mentions selling.

Quite how any long term investor can hope to pick three or four stocks to live with for a lifetime, to forget about for twenty, thirty, forty years eludes me. Even Buffett talks about viewing your investment career like having a punch card. That will allow you only twenty decisions, because you are unlikely to alight upon even that number of Inevitables in a lifetime.

As ever, looking at what the master himself suggests, as distinct from the preachings of those who seek to apply his ideas more widely, it is hard to argue. You do get few chances of finding stocks which will perform for a lifetime. If you do find one, just one, how do you know?

The underlying arrogance of making such an assumption is staggering. Only time can tell. If you have spent six years holding a stock which then goes bust, that is six wasted years. You cannot ask for your money and your time back, apologise, say you made a mistake. It does not work that way. Mere mortal investors make too many mistakes to stand by a decision indefinitely, to ignore it if the share price starts telling you that you have got it wrong.

You cannot buy, file away, and forget. Even the blessed Buffett does not do that. You have to work at investment. If you are not prepared to accept the challenge of running a share portfolio properly, far better to leave it to someone else. Put the money into a general unit trust

> Quite how any long term investor can hope to pick three or four stocks to live with for a lifetime, eludes me.

or investment trust. Or the Tracker funds which Buffett blesses. That way, at least, you spread the risk and have a professional manager watching it all the way for you.

The Truth About The Stock Market

Perhaps the problem is merely one of the names we use. The professionals like to talk about investment. The name the small investor might prefer is gambling. In reality, gambling (speculation is what City types prefer to call it) is what the stock market is about. Forget the pretence of providing money to finance industry. That is what the big boys may be doing. Most small investors, though, are in the market simply to use their money to make money, hoping to pick a share which will generate a greater return than a building society deposit account. Admit that, and you cut through much of the fudge. And the intelligent gambler realises the value of hedging bets, limiting the risk.

That takes it back to common sense. Pick one share, stick with it for years, and you are putting your bet on one runner. Opt for an active investment programme, backed by a decision to sell when things look like going wrong, and you make more choices, place more bets. The active investor might use a Stop Loss system to move the same slug of money through two, three, maybe four stocks in a two year period. That spreads the risk, and raises the chances of spotting one decent winner.

One of the great advantages share trading has over other forms of gambling is that it gives you a second or third chance, maybe more, if you have got it wrong and act quickly enough. You need to be able to sell if it looks as if you have gone wrong, to cut your losses before they waste too much of your stake money.

Betting on BTG may be a very bright idea

By MICHAEL WALTERS

The Stockmarket is a gamble
Daily Mail, 20 November 1995

Hold on by all means while the performance is good. Certainly let your winners run on, year-in, year-out if they deliver performance. But only a Warren Buffett, or some institution investing an awful lot of someone else's

In reality, gambling is what the stock market is about

money, can afford to tolerate poor performers for long.

Never forget, either, that those who trot out charts citing the long term performance of the main share indices may be cheating. They may not realise it but they are. The rise and rise of the indices incorporates a simple selection process, the survival of the fittest if you like. Should one of the big name companies in the index go bust, it is replaced by another. If you are unfortunate enough to have one of your potential twenty year investments go bust on you, that is it. You have lost the lot. You cannot simply slot in a replacement like the index compilers. While top 100 companies do not go under, it gets pretty close. In fairness, no-one following the careful rules for investment operated by value investors like Buffett would have picked either Polly Peck or Maxwell Communication. But both came close to being FTSE-100 companies, and both went under in the early nineties.

They are extreme – but real – examples of the dangers of misguided long term stock selection. While they wiped out their shareholders, the indices chug on, sticking with the winners. As the value of the top companies slips back, those companies drop out of the index, and are replaced by the rising stars, the ones whose market values have been rising. The top 100 companies are not fixed forever. Each quarter, the ones at the bottom are overtaken in value and replaced by the ones which have been rising. The index compilers struggle to explain why, but claim that there is no built-in bias towards superior performance.

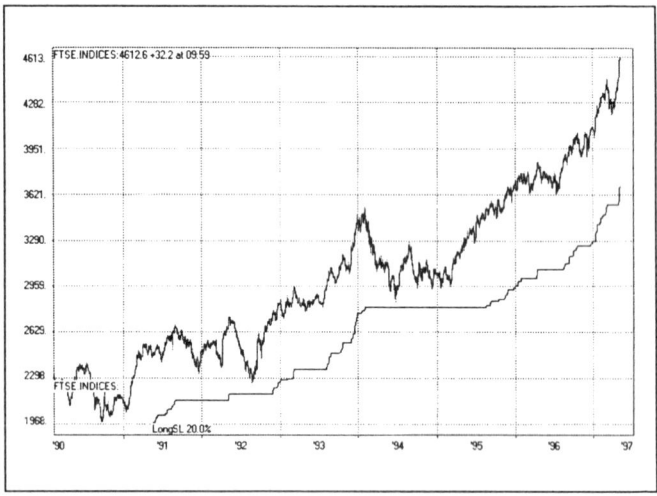

FTSE 100 Share Index 1990-1997 . . . a super-sophisticated Stop Loss system.

Nonetheless, the index does effectively operate a selection process of its own. Because the constituents of the indices are not fixed – how could they be? – they involve an involuntary form of investment management. They effectively stick with the winners, filter out the losers – a sort of super-sophisticated Stop Loss system.

Working The System

In essence, almost any serious attempt at making money by investing in equities must be more than just choosing the right stocks to buy. It must also involve taking decisions to sell at some point. The most committed, longest-term value investors cannot ignore the need to sell something at some point, to take profits or cut losses. They just try not to think about it too hard.

The skill of selling is the neglected half of successful investment. No-one can provide the complete, all-round answer on the way to do it. But it pays to think about it, to work at it. And it pays to have a system.

No system is perfect, but the Stop Loss is much the most valuable simple investment aid I have come across in thirty-five years in the investment world. I have used it in public in print for far longer than anyone I know. In the last few years, I am delighted to see that other newspapers have begun to talk about Stop Loss, even to advocate it for some of their share tips in half-hearted fashion. Some tip sheets have also woken up to it.

> No system is perfect, but the Stop Loss is much the most valuable simple investment aid I have come across in thirty-five years in the investment world.

This Is The System

It is nothing new. Bob Beckman, bless him, introduced me to it thirty years ago. Over that period, I have used it successfully in several subscription-only tip sheets, in the *Daily Mail* in the eighties, and in the *Daily Mail* tipping column I have written for much of the nineties. If you get into the fast-moving, highly-sophisticated world of futures and derivatives, you find Stop Loss levels everywhere. Read either of the Jack Schwager 'Market Wizards' books interviewing top international traders about their techniques (you really should), and you will find constant references to them.

The wonder of the Stop Loss system is that it is easy to follow. You can graft on all sorts of bells and whistles as you choose, and adapt it to suit your own ideas, but in essence, it is terribly simple.

"You should really read this."

System that helps you run your profits and cut losses

AFTER a few nail-gnawing weeks when half the City seemed convinced we were on the brink of higher interest rates, calm has returned. Talk of a share slump has faded, and the boys seem to be gearing up for a good run in September.

Whether it will actually come to pass is impossible to guess. Which brings me to the stop loss, the fail-safe system at the heart of my share tipping progress. If you are familiar with it, I am sorry to bore you.

A whole new batch of readers has been asking

STOP LOSS UPDATE

how it works. Whenever you buy a share, set a price at which you will sell and limit your loss if something goes wrong. If you pay 100p, for example, set the stop loss at, say, 80p. If it falls to 80p, the market is telling you something may be wrong. Sell at 80p, and limit your loss.

You can set the stop loss where you wish — 10pc, 20pc, 50pc below your buying price. It is up to you. My stop loss

points are set according to instinct and the volatility of the shares concerned.

If you have picked a winner, move the stop loss up behind the price. If your 100p purchase goes to 125p, your stop loss should be 105p. If it hits 150p, your stop loss should be 130p, and so on. Move the stop loss up behind the price, never down.

The system is not perfect. You never sell at the very top, and sometimes you will sell a winner just before it starts to come good. Crucially, it prompts you to run your profits and cut

your losses, the key to successful investment.

No matter how well you might think you are doing, paper profits are for the birds. No profit ever counts until you have sold, and banked your winnings.

Everyone loves to hang on to losers, hoping they will come right. Do not do it. Successful selling is vital, yet often neglected. It warrants a full chapter in all of my investment books.

The freedom to sell quickly is the greatest advantage the private investor has over the big City players. Make the most of it.

A Stop Loss update
Daily Mail, 10 August 1996

> *WHENEVER YOU BUY A SHARE, SET A PRICE AT WHICH YOU WILL SELL SHOULD THAT SHARE FALL. SET THAT SELLING PRICE, SAY, 10% TO 20% BELOW THE BUYING PRICE. NEVER REDUCE IT.*
>
> *AS THE SHARE MOVES UP, MOVE THE STOP LOSS PRICE UP, PENNY FOR PENNY, BEHIND THE PRICE. IF THE SHARE THEN FALLS BACK TO THE INCREASED STOP LOSS PRICE, SELL IT.*

Buy a share at, say, 100p. If you decide that you are prepared to take a loss of 20%, but no more, set your Stop Loss at 80p. Do not waver. If the price falls to 98p on the next day, stick at 80p with the Stop Loss. Never lower it. Should the price slide to 80p, sell. The 20p loss will be painful, but not critical. You will have 80p left to try again in something new.

If your share rises, you use the trailing Stop Loss. Simply trail your Stop Loss price up behind the price, as it goes. So if your 100p share moves up 5p to 105p, raise your Stop Loss by 5p to 85p. When it goes, say, another 7p higher to 112p, lift your Stop Loss point by another 7p to 92p. A 20p rise to 120p means you put your Stop Loss up to 120p, so if the share falls back to 100p, that is when you sell, at break-even.

When the shares hit 150p, you should be trailing your Stop Loss price up to 130p. Your 50p profit looks good, but there may be much more to come. If not, and the price falls, sell at 130p, clinching a 30p profit – still pretty good. By the time your share doubles, hitting 200p, your Stop Loss is 180p. And so on, hopefully onwards and upwards.

That, in a nutshell, is the Stop Loss system. Nothing too complicated. Anyone can follow it, provided they can keep track of share price changes. Commit yourself to it, and you never need face a really painful share loss again, unless you are really unlucky. And you will always take profits on your big winners before they turn sour, unless you are really unlucky.

'Really unlucky' means that you have picked one of the few public company shares which goes bust completely out of the blue – and though some do go bust, hardly any do it without the share price starting to slip first to alert you to the possibility that there is a problem. Or you are holding a share where some really bad news catches the market by surprise, and the shares are marked down very sharply, crashing through your Stop Loss level before you can act. That happens from time to time. There is nothing you can do about it. You should still sell, even if you get much less than your Stop Loss price. Bad news has a nasty habit of getting worse.

No-one ever buys a share with the view to losing money on it. The prudent investor, or perhaps the one who has been burnt a few times, recognises the possibility. We all make mistakes. Some stocks will go wrong. And even with the winners, it is important to have some kind of discipline to guide you on when to take profits.

So do not consider setting a Stop Loss price as an advance admission of defeat. Look upon it as a sensible guide to when you should take your winnings, so that you can move on to another money-making opportunity.

Nothing is chiselled in stone, except the rule that you should never lower your Stop Loss point. Lower your Stop Loss point, and you have lost all reason for the system. It is there to take the emotion out of selling shares, to stop you trying to persuade yourself that this time is different, this time there will be a rally if only you hold on for a few weeks more. Do not do it.

That apart, you can tinker with the system, adapt it to suit your needs in a host of ways. When you buy, you can set the Stop Loss point wherever you think fit. As a rough guide, I usually opt for between 10% and 20% below the buying price, unless the share is particularly volatile, or the market is unusually thin. Hopefully, before buying, you will have watched the price for a while, and got some sort of feel for the way it moves. Shares do tend to develop a pattern. Some move in small steps, others in big bites. Some churn around for a spell, then the price breaks up or down quite sharply.

Take this into account when setting your Stop Loss. That will be governed, of course, by how much risk you are ready to take, how large a loss you will accept before getting out.

In practice, though you will work from your actual buying price as a base, it is hard to keep track using anything but the middle price, the price quoted in the newspapers and on many screens. Clearly there is no point in setting a 20% Stop Loss in a low-priced penny share which moves in big bites. That could mean you are stopped out very quickly.

If you buy a share for $2^1/_2$p, the dealing spread may be $2^1/_4$p to sell, $2^3/_4$p to buy. A Stop Loss price 20% below your $2^1/_2$p price would be 2p. A penny share could move from $2^1/_2$p to 2p in one bite. Certainly it would take only two down moves – first to $2^1/_4$p, then to 2p, and you would find you have hit your Stop Loss price, and you are selling almost before the action has started.

On low-priced shares, then, it makes sense to allow a Stop Loss level maybe 40% or 50% below your buying price. That could prove an important aid in deciding whether you should buy such a share in the first place. Calculating an acceptable Stop Loss margin is likely to bring home to you the dangers of

> Lower your Stop Loss point, and you have lost all reason for the system.

playing in penny shares. Get them right, and there are big rewards. Get them wrong, and you could find you have lost a big chunk of your investment remarkably quickly.

The penny share danger helps us focus on another aspect of the system. Our crude examples ignore the dealing costs – brokers' commission and transfer stamp when you buy – and the market-maker's spread between buying and selling prices. In practice, you can only really track the system using middle prices. So setting a Stop Loss 20% below your buying price understates the potential loss you face if things go wrong, and the profit you realise when selling a winner.

The Importance Of Dealing Spreads

So it is important to consider dealing spreads when you buy. In reasonably active markets, a share which costs around 100p should be tradeable on a buying spread of no more than 4p, maybe less. When you set a Stop Loss at 80p, you are effectively saying you will sell at 78p, assuming a dealing spread of 78p to 82p. You may be able to do better, 79p to 81p.

If you have picked a particularly active share, one where there is good liquidity, with perhaps four or five market-makers trading in reasonable size, with a narrow spread between buying and selling prices, you might find it more suitable to set a relatively tight Stop Loss margin, say 10%. That can make sense if you are trading an especially active stock, or one which is relatively active but has a fairly heavy share price.

If you pick a share which trades at, say 600p, you might find setting a 20% margin is too great. That would involve selling on a fall to 480p. Some such stocks trade on a 8p or 10p spread between buying and selling prices, and you can deal fairly freely in a reasonable number. A fall of 10% might indicate a change of fortune, and you might consider any fall below 540p would be a sell sign. Alternatively, this might be a case for a 15% margin – setting the Stop Loss at 510p. It is up to you, though finessing the system in this way does require an extra commitment to detail, and the ability to watch prices and monitor company news fairly closely.

Ultimately, the decision on selling margins is yours to make. The careful investor will take the dealing spread, price volatility, and the liquidity of the market into consideration when deciding what to buy. Setting the Stop Loss margin has the virtue that it make sure you consider all of these factors, and think carefully about your investment – another way in which running a Stop Loss system helps make you a better investor.

Fine-tuning the selling margin also comes into play when you have a winning share. Buy at 100p, enjoy a rise to 200p, and your Stop Loss should have been trailed up to 180p. Simple enough. But it need not necessarily work that way.

Once you have a big winner, you might choose to approach it differently. The 20% selling margin you built in when you bought at 100p is down to a 10% margin by the time the market price has risen to 200p. At that stage, you might consider giving your winner a little more running room. Think carefully. Perhaps you would feel happier restoring your opening 20% margin, raising it from 20p to 40p a share, and re-setting the 180p Stop Loss price at 160p. Experience tells me that people hate selling winners too soon.

The papers quote middle prices.
Daily Mail, 13 May 1997

Making such a switch does involve breaking the cardinal rule – lowering the Stop Loss level. In general, it is not to be recommended. I prefer to widen the Stop Loss margin by trailing the Stop Loss price up more slowly as shares move higher. Instead, say, of moving the Stop Loss from 180p to 185p as the share price rises to 205p, leave it at 180p. And leave it, perhaps, until your investment rises to 220p. You will not have cut the Stop Loss, simply not trailed it up so aggressively. Once your share starts moving again – say from 220p to 230p – then set the Stop Loss moving again, raising it to 190p.

> **At the risk of boring a few people, it is worth outlining again just how the system works. Every time you buy, set a price at which you will sell and limit your loss. Normally, set it between 10pc and 20pc below your buying price. Never move it down. If the price falls to the stop loss level, you have probably picked the wrong stock at the wrong time. Sell.**
>
> **If the price moves up from your buying level, raise the stop loss accordingly. So if you buy at 100p and set a stop loss at 85p, raise it to 95p if the shares rise to 110p. And so on.**

A Walters warning
Daily Mail, 15 March 1993

Alternatively, you might prefer to keep the Stop Loss a constant percentage behind the price, once you have some paper profits to play with. At 220p, say, a 20% Stop Loss margin would amount to 44p, so your Stop Loss price would be 176p. And at 250p, it would be 50p, for a 200p Stop Loss.

Tinkering can work both ways. There is no need simply to loosen stop levels. If the market in general starts to look trickier, you can tighten the Stop Loss, reducing it from, say, 20% to 15%. Or even 10%.

It is a policy I have often used in my *Daily Mail* column. When the market mood grows uncertain, I move Stop Loss levels up closer behind the share prices, so that readers will sell more quickly on any setback. Though it has been easier to make money in the mid-nineties, profits are never that easy to come by. Guard them carefully. Do not let them simply slip away.

One of the few half-serious pieces of advice on selling which has won a popular following is the notion that once you have doubled your money in a share, sell half. That way, the idea goes, you have retrieved your initial investment, and the shares you keep cost you nothing. The perfect risk-free share. Terrific. Or is it?

Far be it from me to discourage anyone from taking a profit whenever they feel it is best to do so. Safety first, every time. But selling half is really not so sensible by comparison with a proper Stop Loss policy. The Stop Loss encourages you to make the most of a big winner, keeping the largest possible exposure to the upside, while limiting the downside. Bid winners are hard enough to find, and they gain a momentum of their own. Once they start flying, they are apt to keep rising beyond the point of strict value. The market always tends to overdo things, on the upside as well as the down. So sitting tight and enjoying the ride is to be encouraged. Use a trailing Stop Loss, and you may be able to squeeze extra profit out without any significant extra risk.

Take a simple example, using BTG, one of my successful *Daily Mail* tips. Assume you bought at 113p, as recommended, and found yourself looking happily at a price of 226p a few months later. If you bought 1,000 shares, you would have invested £1,130 (ignore expenses for this example). After the shares had doubled, you would have had £2,260. Selling half would have left you with 500 shares, and £1,130 cash.

At the time of writing, BTG shares have been over 690p, some 18 months after being tipped. But, lest anyone accuse me of over-egging the pudding, let us assume a price of 600p. If you had sold half, you would be holding 500 shares worth £3,000, and you would have taken out £1,130 cash, for a total of £4,130, and a profit on the deal, so far, of £3,000. Pretty good.

If, however, you had held BTG – in line with the Stop Loss system as updated reguarly in the Daily Mail – you would have had shares woth £6,000 – a profit of £4,870. Your profit would have been more than 50pc greater. Obviously, the higher the BTG price rises, the better it looks for the investor who has held on.

And what if BTG had not proved quite such a good thing. What if BTG had risen to 280p, then tumbled below 226p, say to 200p?

The Stop Loss would still have proved a winner. Assume you were running a fairly conservative Stop Loss, trailing it up 40p below the share price. When the price was 226p, this would have been a margin of close to 20pc – pretty cautious. By the time the price reached 280p, the Stop Loss point would have been up to 240p. If you had sold then, you would have realised £2,400. If you had sold half at 226p, and the rest at 240p, you would have realised £2,320.

Holding the lot and safeguarding the gain with a sensible Stop Loss system would have squeezed out an extra £80 profit. You would have done better, without any real additional risk.

In fact, you might have done very much better. If you were simply operating a sell half system, the chances are that you would still have been holding the remaining half (500 BTG shares) when they were down to 200p. Opting for the idea that your 500 BTG had cost you nothing because you sold half, you might have thrown away the Stop Loss discipline altogether, and risked frittering all of your profit away. Daft.

Cutting The Risks

You may love the idea of a system which does much of your investment thinking for you, or you may hate it. Certainly it destroys the romantic notion that you can develop a special nose for situations, a feel which will somehow ensure that you get things right. Sadly, that can prove to be nothing more than a romantic dream. Instinct is great, and can help you pick winners. When it comes to selling, I promise you, nothing beats a system which kills the romance, and substitutes cold logic.

Even then, you have to work at it, watching price movements closely. In the real world, somehow things never quite work the way you may think they should.

Any investment system gets tested by reality. Then you find the breaking point. There should be just one guarantee attached to each and every system – the promise that sometimes it will go wrong.

Nonetheless, the Stop Loss system is worth working on. I know it makes sense, because I have used it for so long. And used it in my *Daily Mail* columns, where everyone can see it in action. Perhaps it will help to outline a few of the lessons it has taught me.

"Every working day I monitor the price of all the shares I have recommended.'

Every working day, I monitor the price of all of the shares I have recommended. Sometimes it becomes clear that I have made a mistake. Sometimes I have tipped a share which is not performing as I would have hoped. Or perhaps some new factor has emerged to influence trading. In a rising market, it can be wrong simply to issue a sell warning. My judgement is far from perfect. If the stock is rising, even though I am uneasy, why not take advantage of the trend? From time to time, I simply push the Stop Loss level close up behind the price, so that if a buoyant mood should bring any further gain, investors benefit. But if there should be a down-turn, they sell quickly.

> When it comes to selling, nothing beats a system which kills the romance, and substitutes cold logic.

That helps explain what appear to be inconsistencies which sometimes trouble readers of my portfolio. Some stocks have a 20% margin, others practically none at all. In some cases, of course, this arises because some stocks have fallen back, and are moving down towards the Stop Loss selling point.

The Importance Of Daily Monitoring

Ideally, perhaps, you should follow prices daily, and move your Stop Loss levels accordingly. In my newspaper portfolio I am often pressed for space, and can only update my Stop Loss table every four or five weeks. Because of this, it acts only as a general guide. Readers trailing Stop Losses up behind prices will sometimes shift their Stop Loss levels above those in the paper as stocks hit new peaks, so they sell at higher prices than appear in print.

In practice, I find that publishing the table at relatively long intervals is not always a bad thing. It may be best not to rush the Stop Loss up fast behind a rising share price. It may be best to wait a few days, even a week or two. Some prices tend to move in fits and starts. It may be sensible to allow them to consolidate their position, to trade around new heights for a few days, before raising stop levels. That way, you might avoid selling too soon, missing further gains on a big winner which has a flurry, slips back, and only later rises more substantially.

This pin-points the biggest problem with the system. It can take you out of winners too soon, and can prompt you to sell losers just at the point of recovery.

Sadly, there is no way around this. You have to accept it as the price for playing safe, a kind of investment insurance policy. If it happens to you, try to be patient. Measure the money it has saved by taking you out of losers before they got too damaging. And ask yourself whether you set your Stop Loss level correctly in the first place.

My *Daily Mail* columns have featured a few examples of premature Stop Loss ejaculation. Two, in particular, appear unfortunate at first sight. In February, 1996, I recommended English National Investment Company (ENIC) at 48p. I knew Daniel Levy, the managing director, of old, and respected his ability and determination to develop the business. My faith was justified. He bought a stake in an Internet search engine company called Autonomy. The ENIC price topped 105p, but because I was away at the time, my published Stop Loss price never rose above 78p.

Share	Date	Price then	Price now	Stop loss	Action
Abtrust New Dawn	Oct 5	98p	180p	—	sell
Alliance Trust	Oct 12	1350p	1759p	1689p	rsl
P&O	Oct 26	438p	669p	646p	rsl
Abtrust New Thai	Nov 9	83p	114p	—	sell
Standard Chartered	Nov 23	570p	884p	859p	rsl
BTR 1997 wts	Dec 7	68p	138p	119p	rsl
Royal Bank of Scot	Mar 22	254½p	298p	269p	rsl
Avesco	Apr 4	86p	102p	88p	rsl
BAT	Apr 13	443p	453p	405p	rsl
Scotia	Apr 19	390p	suspended	—	hold
Suter	Apr 26	139p	176p	156p	rsl
Suter wts	Apr 26	free	49p	31p	rsl
Invesco	Jun 7	118p	158p	140p	rsl
Caldwell	Jun 14	39p	38p	32p	hold
Burnfield	Jul 19	143p	138p	120p	hold
Mosaic	Jul 19	15p	17p	11p	rsl
Barratt	Jul 26	149p	158p	131p	rsl

(rsl means raise stop loss)

Michael Walters share table.
Daily Mail, 9 August 1993

Autonomy appeared to have teething troubles. Exceptionally, because I knew the company well, I cut my Mail Stop Loss point modestly to 75p when it began to drift in the autumn of 1996.

Why English National looks a grand gamble

By MICHAEL WALTERS

KEEP on worrying. As Wall Street whizzes ahead to record after record, and London hovers close to the peak, the chorus of dithering sceptics wails in the background. They warn that a crash could come, but few are quite brave enough to say just when.

The doomsters have been at it for years. Anyone who heeded them and kept out of shares has been very badly advised, missing splendid profit opportunities. Of course, markets will turn down eventually. They might crash. It could even happen quite soon. But there is no need to be totally negative. That way, you never

holds 29pc of suction house Christie's and 10pc of tiny property group Harmony.

He has few plans for ENIC himself, and is simply backing managing director Daniel Levy and his board. I chanced on Levy a decade ago as a bright young man learning his way around the investment scene. Now in his early thirties, he has proved his worth to Lewis, gaining his support in sorting out and rebuilding businesses. He is eager to succeed at ENIC, and is likely to abandon investment trust status and convert it into a trading company when the right deal comes along. Net asset value is 34p.

There is no timetable, simply a determination to move cautiously and wait for the right deal. At 48p, the shares can be traded in lots of 5,000 or

profits looks within sight this year. The shares sell on 31-times prospective earnings. It would be foolish to forbid taking profits, but hold if you can. There is more to come yet.

BTG goes from strength to strength, up from 585p in November to 1248p as institutions begin to understand better the enormous wealth of patents and possibilities in the group.

Last week, it clinched another nice little earner as international giant Bausch & Lomb signed to make and sell Award daily disposable contact lenses. BTG helped to fund the technology, patenting and licensing strategy.

Quality Care Homes produced excellent results for the year to October 31, with pre-tax profits up from

"Premature Stop Loss ejaculation"
Daily Mail, 19 February 1996

It carried on drifting, and readers were advised to take their profits at 75p. Months later, again while I was on holiday, the action happened. ENIC bought a large stake in Rangers, the leading Scottish football club. The shares leapt to 267$\frac{1}{2}$p. Investigating the company, I recommended the shares a second time, suggesting readers buy at 209p.

The Story Of Shield Diagnostics

Something similar happened with Shield Diagnostic. This modest Dundee developer of diagnostic kits looked cheap to me at 67p in August 1995. It seemed that one product in particular, a test to identify

Activated Factor Twelve in the blood, could emerge as a superior indicator of impending heart disease. Extensive tests were being carried out, in Houston and in this country under supervision of doctors at St Bartholomew's Hospital in London. These tests, and the reporting of their results, were not under the company's control. As the wait for results dragged on, the shares became unsettled, and they dropped through my Stop Loss. Readers were advised to sell at 140p in July 1996. Anyone who followed my advice would have doubled their money in just over a year. At one point, the shares had topped 180p, so sharp sellers might have almost trebled their money. No regrets, though. The system had worked, and worked well.

It looked particularly astute when Shield shares dropped below 115p briefly in the autumn of 1996 as the company issued a warning that profits would be a touch disappointing. The market, still waiting for progress on the AFT test, misread that as a general warning, and marked the shares down sharply.

Early in 1997, excitement began to build again. Shield had circulated a newsletter to the medical profession and to City analysts. It contained encouraging comments from doctors about the AFT test. In effect, several said it worked well, a view which was confirmed by the company. In a few weeks in February, the shares rocketed from 130p to well over 500p.

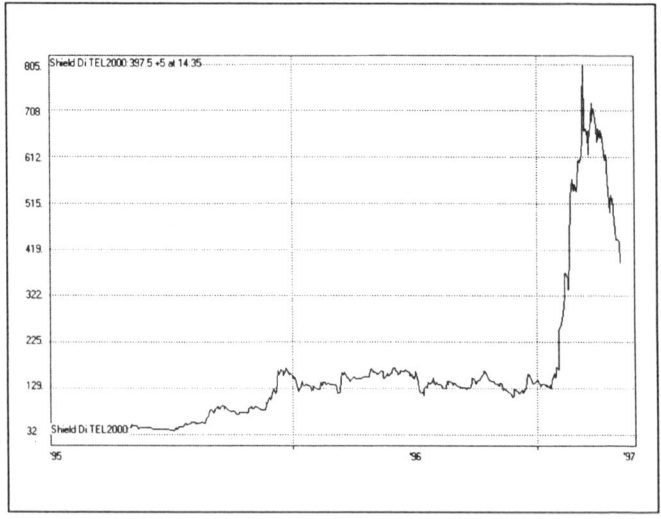

Shield Diagnostics 1995-1997
Source: Updata Investment

I started looking at Shield again, and concluded that the Activated Factor Twelve test looked almost certain to replace cholesterol tests as the leading indicator of heart disease. I recommended the shares again at 529¹/₂p, more than three times above the price at which I had said sell. As ever, there could be no guarantees. But if the AFT test worked as well as seemed probable, and won even a 10% share of the market from cholesterol tests, profits could hit £30m at some stage, all being well. So Shield shares might be worth very much more than 529¹/₂p.

Of course it would have looked smarter to have told everyone to stay aboard both ENIC and Shield all of the way up – a real triumph if readers who had bought

Shield at 67p were still aboard when they hit 920p briefly in March 1997.

On reflection, though, there was nothing to be sorry about. There is nothing to say you cannot buy back in to a share which you have sold. It is something I have done quite frequently in my tipping column over the past four years. By the time I returned to ENIC and Shield, much of the initial uncertainty had gone, both companies had moved on significantly, and were much safer propositions than when they were first recommended. That is one of the key and most exciting elements of share investment. Companies do change, they evolve, Sometimes they grow, sometimes they shrink. There is nothing inevitable about the process. That makes winners, and losers. No-one was exposed to the months of 'ifs' and 'buts' as ENIC looked for a big deal, and Shield waited and waited for the official AFT test results. The hesitation may seem silly now with the benefit of hindsight. But ENIC could have continued to drift back, and might not have done the Rangers deal. Shield had a rapid run to 920p after my second tip, then plunged to 520p in twenty minutes late one Friday afternoon as it reported that blood clotting in ten-year-old test samples had hampered the Houston test. Happily, results from other tests are highly encouraging. But what if the real tests had turned out badly, after all?

In each case, the Stop Loss system took investors out with a handsome profit, removed them from the risk of something going wrong, and freed capital for re-investment.

Tring International – "thank goodness for the Stop Loss system"
Daily Mail, April 18 1994

Those sales proved premature. Others worked wonderfully. In April 1994, I recommended Tring International, a small specialist in low-priced compact discs. I knew the people behind it, and had recommended backing their skills successfully in the eighties. The shares had not long been floated, and had got off to a weak start in the face of what appeared to be ill-judged criticism. After I tipped them, they began to rise nicely, moving from 124p to 151p. The Stop Loss price trailed up to 126p. Then they began to slide. In September 1994, just five months after I tipped them, I advised readers to sell at 126p, a tiny nominal profit. After expenses, readers took a small loss, but came to no great harm. Crucially, they got their cash out of a non-performer after just five months, freeing it to put into something more dynamic.

Tring carried on down. Management problems emerged, and although the initial criticisms proved largely unjustified, the business went from bad to worse, and the share price with it. The shares hit 12¹⁄₂p in 1996. Thank goodness for the Stop Loss.

A Sorry Tale: Memory Corporation

Then there was Memory Corporation. This company had developed exciting technology for using defective microchips in a way which overcame their faults. Chip prices were soaring, demand was vastly in excess of supply, and Memory could use chips which were virtually being dumped as waste, then sell them at extremely good prices.

I tipped the shares first at 210p in June 1995. They went up and up. Come September, with the price at 460p, I looked closely at prospects again. They appeared excellent. I recommended the shares a second time.

Then the inevitable – or what sometimes seems like it – happened. Everything that had looked so right started to go wrong. Chip prices began to ease. The gentle fall became a crash. And Memory hit delays in getting its own system operational. The share price, which initially carried on up after my second tip, began to slip. Because I had been away, I had moved my *Daily*

Mail Stop Loss price up slowly, and missed the best of the gain. The shares fell through my Stop Loss at 380p in January, 1996. Readers who had bought on my initial recommendation were advised to sell at a gain of 81% in seven months. Those who followed the second tip took a loss of 17% in four months.

The disappointment was nothing compared to what was to follow. As demand for chips suddenly slacked and prices tumbled ever lower, Memory shares went into reverse. At one stage they touched 35p amid real questions about the viability of the business. This brilliant bit of British technology only really made money when chips were in short supply, and prices were high. The company has survived, and could yet have a profitable future, but the going looks tough. In each case, my readers have cause to bless the Stop Loss system. Perhaps some ignored it, and held on in hope. They have paid dearly. Others have written to say that they never sold their Shield when they fell through the Stop Loss, and are now sitting on ten times their money. They have triumphed.

In retrospect, I have no regrets, although obviously I am sorry that any shares I have tipped should have gone down, even after I advised selling. It seems that I might have raised the Stop Loss price on ENIC too quickly, given that the shares were a relatively tight market, and moved fairly sharply on relatively low trade. But then I did not raise the Stop Loss level as quickly as I might have done

> My readers have cause to bless the Stop Loss system.

when the price pushed up over 100p. I did move the Stop Loss price on Tring up fairly quickly, partly because I grew uneasy about the continuing barrage of criticism directed towards the company, even though I believed it was misplaced.

It all emphasises that my judgement was less than perfect, even though I research any companies I recommend very closely, and try to track events carefully. The Stop Loss system, too, was less than perfect. It succeeded brilliantly, though, in saving investors from the consequences of my mistakes. In every case, losses were cut or profits taken pretty promptly when things began to turn down. Vitally, it prevented faults in my judgement doing much damage, and stopped me from encouraging readers to stay aboard and hope there would be a turn for the better.

> The Stop Loss system, succeeded brilliantly in saving investors from the consequences of my mistakes.

The system did its job. It prompted readers to move on quickly, and freed the cash to try again. Events at ENIC, Shield, Tring and Memory illustrate the extremes. Other examples run more smoothly.

Michael Walters' Record

Between October 1992 and February 1997, I recommended around 100 shares in the *Daily Mail*. Only four have been sold with losses greater than 20%, and three of those were special situations. I cannot remember why the fourth – Tarmac with a 25% loss –

went wrong. The biggest loss was 36% in AIM tiddler Thomas Potts, where the price ran up sharply between writing the piece and it appearing in the newspaper. Knowing a deal was being negotiated, and hoping that would retrieve it, I left a substantial margin on this speculative stock. The deal fell through, and the price tumbled. It has since regained the original tipped price, but in nearly two years after the tip, we are still waiting for a deal. The other big loss was a 33% fall in bio-tec specialist Scotia, which I spotted well before it came to the official market, and tipped with heavy warnings about risk. It made a shaky start on the main market, and that sparked the Stop Loss sale. Later it raced ahead, only to lose much of the gain. The vast bulk of the tips have scored gains between 10% and 90%, many in under a year, before being Stop Lossed out as they lost momentum. Several did double, but because the Stop Loss trails up behind the rise, the actual profits on selling are below what some investors might have made. This may make the tips look less exciting, but that does not matter. What really counts is buying and then selling, the profits you take, not the ones you just miss.

What the system has done well, in addition to containing the downside, is that it has encouraged readers to stay with winners, and make big gains. Several tips have doubled, trebled, quadrupled, or even better, often inside a year, almost always within two years. Utility Cable, for example, went from the equivalent to 6p to 30p in eight months, Unipalm from 118p to 500p in six months, Tepnel from the equivalent to 15p to 60p in 13 months. At the time of writing, the portfolio is sitting with Biocompatibles up from 352p to over 1,420p in eight months,

> What the system has done well, in addition to containing the downside, is that it has encouraged readers to stay with winners, and make big gains.

Hay & Robertson from 36p to 145p in 18 months, BTG from 113p to 660p in 17 months, and Tepnel (second time around) from 37½p to 115p in six months.

Scotia's evening primrose may bring a bright dawn

HOW would it be if you could buy shares in one of our most exciting pharmaceuticals companies, with a portfolio of promising new drugs in the development stage? And if you could pick them up before the hip hooray and hoopla of a full public flotation?

Getting in first is risky, of course. Merely writing about it here means that it could well be difficult for everyone to deal. And there is a risk that the price could run away to ridiculous levels.

Approach it with your eyes open, though, and you might want to try. This column mixes big, relatively safe share recommendations — the likes of the Prudential and BAT — with altogether more speculative ideas.

Readers who chide me for repeatedly emphasising the risks misunderstand my intention — I am not hedging my bets, simply trying to make sure that everyone realises that share deals are risky, and some are much riskier than others.

Scotia – Warning
Daily Mail, 18 April 1994

Several of those companies are in the bio-technology business. Others in high tech. Yet more are relatively modest companies, growth stocks in the early stages of development.

A Stock Market Crash

It would have been irresponsible to recommend them without also providing some form of damage limitation, something which reduced the risks to readers if the tips turned out wrong. Not all of my tips were small or speculative situations, however, though small to medium companies have generated the majority of my gains. Even the biggest boys came with a recommended Stop Loss price. Anything else would have been wrong. Who was to say that there might not have been a stock market crash, sending shares plunging? When I started tipping again in October 1992, many were worried that our exit from the ERM was bad news. It could trigger runaway inflation, bringing economic catastrophe.

By the spring of 1994, the world and his wife was predicting a plunge in share prices. Wall Street, commentators galore agreed, was overstretched. It was sure to crash before long. The spring of 1995 brought similar fears. They surfaced again in the following year.

Yet all of the time, share prices rose. London and Wall Street hit one new high after the other. The stock market was booming, despite the Jeremiahs. What those gloomsters cost their followers in terms of lost opportunities it hard to calculate. Anyone who sat with their money in a deposit account, waiting for the fall, missed some brilliant money-making opportunities.

So far as I am concerned, it was only possible to exploit them with some sort of risk limitation plan in the background. It does take nerve to buy shares when pundits all around are predicting trouble. And this, perhaps, is the greatest virtue of the Stop Loss. Because it takes the difficult selling decisions, it cuts the risks, frees you to move into the market when others are staying away, scared of a fall.

Overcoming Inertia

It dies hard, the notion that long term investment is proper, and anything short term is reckless. Inevitably, suggestions that trading in and out of shares actually reduces risk and can produce superior results will be greeted with scorn, claims that it is simply not worthwhile. If active investment does exploit market volatility, any gains it might generate are gobbled up by extra costs, the argument goes.

Perhaps. My *Daily Mail* column has ignored the matter of costs, partly because tackling them would take up too much valuable space, partly because I do not have time to calculate them, and partly because they complicate a system which some struggle to understand in any event.

The Issue Of Costs

Let us try to tackle them. There are several different costs in share dealing. When you buy, you pay commission to the broker, and stamp duty of 0.5% of the cost of the shares to the Government. There is a small levy on bigger deals. When you sell, you simply pay commission to the broker. You can shop around for a broker. A good broker is worth every penny he will charge. Ideally, you will develop a mutual trust which will help him understand what you are trying to do, and to exchange ideas with you. A good broker will often be able to deal inside the prices shown on the TV screens, and if he can save you ½p on 1,000 shares, that means £5 for you. If he saves it on 5,000 shares, that is £25. So think hard before you opt for trading through a low commission house which offers a cheap, execution only service. The £15 you save in commission may be a false economy.

You can trade in smaller lots for £9 commission if you pay an annual fee of under £25, or for £16.50 on deals up to £1m for a £96 annual fee. Assume, then, that you pay commission at £25 for deals up to £5,000, and £40 for deals between £5,000 and under £10,000, and £50 for deals over that.

This means that, when you invest £1,000 in a share, you might spend £25 on commission, and £5 in stamp duty, for a total buying cost of £30. Do well, double your money, and sell, and you spend a further £25 in commission. So your total buying and selling cost is £55. Your share gain is £1,000, and your overall profit after buying and selling costs is £945.

Assume you top your stake money up to £2,000, and re-invest. Once again, you will incur commission of £25. Stamp duty will be £10. Assume you make a 50% gain this time, taking your capital to £3,000. That would incur a selling commission of £25. Your total dealing costs on this second little winner amount to £60. You would have made £940 on your second investment, after expenses. Total profits £1,885, after total costs of £115. Since you put in an extra £55 to top up the capital after the first deal, the real profit would be £1,830.

Sounds good. But that does not tell the full story. The biggest cost is not really in commission and stamp duty. It is in the spread, the difference between the buying price and selling price of your shares. If you are buying a share which costs under 100p, this spread could easily be 4% or 5%. Take a middle price of 100p, and the real dealing levels might be 97½p to sell, and 102½p to buy.

Assume you buy 1,000 shares. That will cost £1,025, plus £25 commission, plus stamp duty of £5.12 making a total investment of £1,055.12. The middle price of the shares doubles, going from 100p to 200p. The dealing spread might well still be 5p, or 197½p to sell, 202½p to buy. When you sell, then, you would realise £1,975, and pay £25 commission, so you would receive £1,950.

In our earlier example, ignoring the spread, this

meant a notional profit of £945. In reality, the profits after all expenses is likely to be £894.88. Obviously the real deal has not been so favourable, but it still looks pretty good.

Once again, re-working the earlier example, assume you top up your capital, and invest £2,000 in shares which gain 50%. If you are to buy 1,000 shares, you will need to top your capital up to £2,025 to cover the dealing spread. There will be commission of £25, and stamp duty of £11.25, so the full cost amounts to £2,061.25. By the time the middle price has risen to 300p, the real price might have widened a touch, say to 297p to sell, 303p to buy. So when you sell, you will actually get £2,970, minus £25 commission, for a total of £2,945. So your profit on the second deal amounts to £873.75. Total profits on the two sets of deals amounts to £1,668.63, minus the £166.37 extra capital put in to top up for the second purchase. So the total gain is £1,502.26.

That is quite a discount on the quick, easy notion that, if you start with £1,000, double it, and then make a further 50% gain on a second deal, you have made £2,000. The long term investors might suggest you would have been better off simply staying put, hoping for the day when your original £1,000 investment would have been worth £3,000 without the expense and trouble of extra deals.

That, though, would also be misleading. Even assuming you had picked a share which would eventually perform that well, there would have been dealing costs. The original purchase would have incurred commission and stamp duty of £5.12, and would have had to take in the dealing spread. So the initial £1,000 would have cost £1,055.12, regardless of how long you intend to hold. And the selling costs when the price had trebled would be exactly the same as for the short term dealer, with commission, and the dealing spread. So the actual cash in hand for when the long term seller takes profits would be £2,945. The gain, after all costs would be £1,889.78. That compares to our £1,502.26 for the trader.

The long term holder, however, has had one chance at making a killing, and had to pick a stock which trebled. The more active dealer had a couple of chances, and had to pick one stock which doubled, and another which gained 50%. Chasing a stock which doubles might be held by orthodox investment opinion to be a less risky business than hunting one which trebles. Looking for a stock which rises 50% appears to adopt a still lower risk. Who knows? Maybe both sides are playing with words, conducting an empty guessing game. But the case for suggesting that the long term player is automatically assuming a lower risk is debatable, at best.

You can play around with figures to produce all sorts of answers, but the reality is that, unless you are dealing excessively, the actual cost of trading sensibly is not excessive. The Stop Loss system is not intended to encourage wild speculation, quite the contrary. It is a sensible way of limiting risk, taking you out of the market when risks rise.

Take a couple of the earlier examples from the Crash of 1987. If you had been running a Stop Loss 15% below the price of ICI (a very conservative strategy for such a large, readily marketable stock), it would have been triggered as the shares fell from 1,583p to 1,346p. Given that the spread on even such a liquid share might have risen to 10p in such conditions (a middle price of 1,346p covering 1,341p to sell, 1,351p to buy), an investor holding 100 shares would have incurred commission of £25, and realised £1,316.

Four months later, the price was 1,045p. Buying back the 100 shares would have cost £1,055.25, after commission of £25 and stamp duty of £5.25. The investor would have been safe in cash for four months of market turmoil, yet able to re-invest with a profit of £260.75 after dealing costs. Seems sensible.

It would be possible to produce all sorts of examples. They are meaningless if you simply pluck them from the air. Let me, then, choose just one out of several I could use from my *Daily Mail* columns. Sceptics should note that I am deliberately using examples which involve a relatively modest investment of £1,000 initially – the kind of sum many small investors might use. If you choose to invest larger amounts, the sums come out more strongly in favour of the active investor. Dealing costs do not rise in direct proportion to the sum invested, so the more you invest, the lower the trading cost proportionately.

Regalian Properties

In March 1993, I suggested buying shares in Regalian Properties, hoping that the recovery in the general housing development market would send them higher. The middle price was 15¼p. The real market quotation for Regalian was 15p to sell, 15½p to buy. Anyone buying 10,000 would have paid £1,550, plus commission of £25, plus stamp duty of £7.75, or a total of £1,582.75.

Share	Date	Price then	Price now	Stop Loss	Action
Abtrust New Dawn	Oct 5	98p	170p	158p	rsl
Alliance Trust	Oct 12	1350p	1633p	1590p	rsl
P&O	Oct 26	438p	583p	553p	hold
Abtrust New Thai	Nov 9	63p	109p	100p	rsl
Prudential	Nov 16	280p	319p	303p	hold
Refuge	Nov 15	713p	1033p	1003p	hold
Standard Chartered	Nov 23	570p	723p	672p	rsl
BTR 1997 wts	Dec 7	113½p	162p	140p	rsl
Greenwich Resources	Feb 20	10p	18½p	16p	rsl
Tadpole Tech	Jan 1	168p	307p	240p	hold
Tadpole Tech	Feb 22	298p	307p	240p	hold
P&P	Mar 15	57p	71p	59p	rsl
Roy Bank of Scot	Mar 22	254½p	272p	235p	rsl
Regalian	Mar 29	15¼p	27p	23p	rsl
Avasco	Apr 4	96p	88p	68p	rsl
BAT	Apr 13	887p	868p	785p	hold
Kewell Systems	Apr 13	136p	152p	128p	rsl
Scotia	Apr 19	780p	800p	560p	buy
Suter	Apr 28	139p	143p	120p	buy
Millwall	May 4	2½p	2¼p	1¼p	buy

Regalian Properties – a Michael Walters Tip.
Daily Mail, 19 April 1993

Regalian shares advanced quickly, touching 27p, then slipping back, and hitting my Stop Loss of 23p late in May of that year, a couple of months later. A sale at 22½p would have realised £2,250, minus £25 commission, for a total of £2,225. That meant a quick gain of £632.25, or almost 40% after all expenses. Not bad.

In July 1995, I returned to Regalian. The company has a stake in a disused goods yard near London's Paddington Station. It could become a massive, and massively profitable, development. The shares had drifted back following my earlier success, and I recommended buying at a middle price of 19p. A purchase of 10,000 for 19½p would have cost £1,984.75 after commission of £25 and stamp duty of £9.75. By August 1996, Regalian was 39p. It seemed fully valued to me. I set myself a mental Stop Loss of 37½p, and as it slipped back, suggested selling at that level. I was pleased that readers could have virtually doubled their money in just over a year. Selling at an actual market price of 37p, with commission charges of £25, anyone who had bought 10,000 would have realised £3,675. The actual realised profit on the deal would have been £1,690.75.

Look back, though, over the series, buying, selling, buying again, and selling again. Anyone who had bought 10,000 on my original suggestion would have paid £1,582.75, and realised £3,675, for a profit of £2,082.25 after all expenses.

Anyone who bought, sold, bought again and sold again would have realised profits of £2,323 after expenses on the trades. And they would have had £230.25 in the bank, the unused difference between the profits taken on the first sale and the cost of buying in a second time. So the total gain was £2,563.25.

Clearly, in this example, there was a substantial advantage to the active trader, who came out with £872.50 more profit – over 50% more profit – than the passive investor who simply sat and waited.

What does this prove? In truth, not very much. It all depends on what figures you use, whether you manage to pick the right shares at the right prices.

All it demonstrates is that the old, old suggestion that the active trader always loses by comparison with a long term trader is not correct. Anyone can make up examples to prove any point. The Regalian example is taken from advice offered to millions of readers in the pages of the *Daily Mail*, as it happened. That cannot be fixed – though other people could choose different examples to arrive at different answers.

In the end, you either believe, or you do not. You are either disposed to become an active trader, trying to play the rises and falls and limiting risk that way. Or you opt for the long term, and become an inert investor, picking a few shares, dozing off, and hoping they turn up nicely in the end.

I know which method I prefer. I know that, no matter how hard I try to get it right every time, I will make mistakes, and that my would-be long term investments will probably stop performing sooner or later. Even Warren Buffett makes mistakes. He can afford to sit with them. The average private investor cannot enjoy that luxury. Even though you must only play the market with money you can afford to lose, it hurts to lose it. If you can retrieve some of it, and try again, that must make sense for most small investors. And that is why the Stop Loss system makes sense.

Seize the opportunity. Play the share market, hunt profits, have fun, and limit your risks with my secret weapon – the Stop Loss system.

Profit From Your PC

In today's turbulent investment market the PC is a resource no serious investor can afford to overlook. *Profit From Your PC* offers guidance on buying a computer and the software options, explains how to capture share data from the Information Superhighway and also covers basic technical analysis, helping you identify which shares to buy and when to sell.

ISBN 0 948035 16 1 Price £9.99 Paperback

'If you only have time to read one book on investment, this is the one'
Mr R Smith, Lancs

'A superb introduction to share investment using a PC'
Mr R Bryans, Berks

More Profit From Your PC

Building on the principles outlined in the best-selling *Profit From Your PC, More Profit From Your PC* offers even more hot tips and practical advice on the great opportunities unfolding for private investors via the Internet.

Bigger, better and with completely up-to-the-minute information, this superb follow-up to *Profit from your PC* may prove to be your greatest asset yet!

ISBN 0 948035 62 5 Price £14.99 Paperback

'. . . a concise all-round guide to the basics of technical analysis . . . as a get you started manual it is one of the best.'
Sunday Times, December 1996

Save £5 when ordering both titles.
See order form for details.

Order Form

BOOK TITLE	PRICE	QUANTITY	COST
Profit From Your PC	£9.99		
More Profit From Your PC	£14.99		
Both PC Titles	£19.99		
How to Make a Killing in Penny Shares	£6.99		
How to Make a Killing in the AIM	£8.99		
How to Make a Killing in the Share Jungle	£9.99		
Michael Walters Triology (All Three Titles)	£23.99		

POSTAGE: In the UK please add £1.50 for the first title ordered plus £1.00 for each extra book (maximum £5.50).
Overseas add £6.00 for the first item plus £5.00 for each extra item (maximum £20.00).

TOTAL

+ P&P

HOW TO ORDER

GRAND TOTAL

YOUR DETAILS

Name: _____

Address: _____

_____

_____

_____

Postcode: _____

Country: _____

Tel: _____

Fax: _____

1 BY CREDIT CARD

Please debit my credit card £ _____

Expiry date ____/____ Mastercard   Visa

Card Number

Or call 01525 850270 quoting your credit card and ref no: WEAPON 1

2 BY CHEQUE

I/We enclose my/our cheque for £ _____

made payable to: **Rushmere Wynne Limited**

Please return this order form to: Rushmere Wynne Limited, FREEPOST ANG 5069, Leighton Buzzard, Bedfordshire, LU7 8Z

Tel: 01525 853726   Fax: 01525 852037